T0103921

POTPOURRI

MERRILL PHILLIPS

Order this book online at www.trafford.com
or email orders@trafford.com

Most Trafford titles are also available at major online book retailers.

Printed in the United States of America.

ISBN: 978-1-4907-2630-4 (sc)
ISBN: 978-1-4907-2631-1 (e)

Trafford rev. 01/28/2014

www.trafford.com

North America & international
toll-free: 1 888 232 4444 (USA & Canada)
fax: 812 355 4082

CONTENTS

A Gift From God

From the hand of God, I was given the gift of writing; it has been and continues to be the greatest experience of my life.

It is not from me that the message comes; it is from God, I just listen and write what He wants me to relay.

At times, it comes in the middle of the night; He awakes me with a thought on my mind and I write. Other times it comes when least expected.

It is a great journey that God has me on, one that I never expected or ever gave a thought.

I am not schooled or trained in what I have come to love to do; I just listen and write whatever He puts on my mind. It is a pleasure to do God's will; I never thought that I ever could.

I can now look back and see things in my past that has prepared me for what He now wants me to do.

Many of life experiences (both good and bad) have contributed to me becoming a writer.

While still in high school I needed another point or two to graduate, He had me take typing lessons and from the start, I wondered why I took such a class, but now I know why He guided me to learn how to type.

I thank God for the gift of writing; it has made my life more fulfilling. In my retirement years, I have had time to publish some of my writings. Hopefully they will be beneficial to those who read them.

CHRISTMAN EVE

---⊗⊗⊗---

The trees were laden with snow their branches' bending to the ground, snow was still falling all around.

Our house was all cozy and warm; flames were dancing in the fireplace, the aroma of the fresh cut Christmas tree filled the air.

With a house full of grandchildren sitting before the open fire, the smell and sound of corn popping while, Grandma fixed the turkey and wild goose for the next day's meal.

Grandpa sitting in his favorite chair before the open fire telling stories of old with the youngest on his knee, they filled the house with love and laughter that Christmas eve.

Grandpa told of how it was the time of year to celebrate the birth of Jesus Christ who came to earth to bring comfort to many a troubled soul, and of how peace, love and salvation was His gift to the whole world.

As darkness fell that Christmas Eve, four little noses pressed against the picture-window pane as they watched Santa make his way across the newly fallen snow.

With eyes wide and excitement in their hearts, they watched as Santa came to the front door and knocked, for from the chimney the smoke of the fire rose high in the cold evening air.

With a Ho Ho Ho Santa entered the house, little ones squealed with delight as Santa settled before the open fire, from his sack of toys, a scroll he took and read each ones name.

With eyes wide they heard Santa tell of how they were naughty and nice, to each he gave a new chore, to help mommy and daddy all year through and be nice, then with a promise of good behavior each one took their place upon his knee.

With love, Santa told them about baby Jesus and His place He should play in their lives; it was a Christmas Eve to remember the rest of their lives.

Then Santa called each one by name, with a hug he gave from his sack, toys, games and good warm clothes for the winter months ahead, with laughter and joy they went off to play with their newly gained toys.

Just as quick as he came Santa went to the door and turned to leave; with a voice of love, he wished each and everyone a merry Christmas as he disappeared into the cold winter night.

Now, those Grandchildren are all grown up and have families of their own, each Christmas eve they gather around the old fireplace and tell the same stories their Grandpa told them that Christmas Eve so long ago.

To all a merry Christmas and goodnight.

CALLED TO SERVE

———⊗⊗⊗———

Another veteran has found eternal rest, another patriot has died, he fought for our freedom during the Great War, and he was a member of the greatest generation.

He sloshed through the muck and mire of the battlefields of World War II and escaped death; he survived because God had other plans for his life.

After the war he married the love of his life and raised his family, at times life was hard but love of family keep his dreams alive.

Never one to shirk his duty he worked the woods and highways of Calhoun County, he tilled the soil and was called to serve the Master of us all.

This turned out to be the reason God spared him from death while serving his country, for now he joined in the greatest war of all, the fight between good and evil.

Bunt spread the word of God to all he met and counseled many a tattered soul and in the process introduced them to the Lord of all, Jesus Christ.

Race, color, or creed mattered not to Bunt, for in everyone he met he saw a child of God who needed to hear the word according to the Scriptures, this was his way of giving back for all the Lord had done for him.

In this, he fought the greatest fight of all, the fight for the souls of all he met, never asking for himself for he knew that God would supply his every need.

Bunt never met a stranger and found it rewarding to spread the word of God to all he met, it kept him young in spirit even though his body showed the scares of battle of both mind and soul.

He has now found his heavenly rest, free from the encumbrances of living in a sin filled world, surly he has reaped the rewards of a soldier of God.

His family and friends will surly miss his sense of humor and forever remember him as a man of peace, one full of the love of God.

Bunt was a farmer of a different kind, he planted the seeds of salvation and watered them with love and compassion, in many cases he lived to see the fruit of his labor and gave all of the credit to God.

A man of peace was he, a stranger he never met, his earthly calling complete he now walks the streets of gold and from every indication he still preaches the word of God and encourages everyone to come before the throne of God and turn their lives over to Him.

Bunt now dwells in God's presence and wants us all to stand firm in the word of the Scriptures and be bold in helping our neighbor seek the shelter of God's omnipotent hand.

Angels Unaware

---⊗⊗⊗---

There are angels among us doing the will of God. They are ordinary people who answer to the call of God whenever and wherever there is a need. They seek not self-recognition or compensation for their deeds for their deeds are done out of love for their fellowman. Often times these angels go unrecognized along with their deeds and thought of as someone who is just doing a favor for a stranger.

Those who do recognize God at work among us know that there is more to these stories than the ordinary people acknowledge. They see God working through those who are willing to let God work through them. Whether in a moment of crisis or a moment of compassion these angels of God express themselves through their deeds of kindness to their fellowman.

I would like to illustrate the work of angels among us through three examples where someone helped their fellowman where at the time others were in need of help in one way or another. These three illustrations are actual events that have taken place in different parts of the country at different times with one common thread; someone was in need of help.

The first event took place on an old woods road that crossed a mountain in the state of New Hampshire. The road was only used in the summertime and was impassable after the first snow of the winter season, for the road was not used enough or wide enough to keep it open during the winter months. If one met a car going in the opposite direction, one or the other had to find a place they could get off the road to allow the other car to pass.

This man lived on one side of the mountain and his place of employment was on the other side of the mountain. He used this mountain road every day to go back and forth to work during the warm months of the year. It saved him many miles a day in his daily commute to and from work. One day while returning home from work, he came across an accident.

A car with two people in it had for whatever reason left the road and turned over. During the accident, both had been thrown from the vehicle. The passenger was dazed, but not hurt seriously. The driver was pinned under the vehicle and her throat had been cut and was bleeding severely. The man could hear the woman breathing while blood was running down her throat, causing a gurgling sound. He knew that she would die if something was not done immediately. His plan of action was to lift the car off the woman while the passenger pulled the woman out from under the car. As he described it later, at that moment he felt an urge of strength, backed up to the front of the car, and lifted the car off the woman while the passenger pulled the woman from under the car. The man took his shirt off, applied it to the bleeding wound, and slowed the bleeding. They then put the woman into his car and drove to where she received life saving help. No one could explain how this man had lifted the car that weighted over a thousand pounds, except to say that it had to be divine intervention.

The second incident is as follows;

A local church was having a fish fry and the Men's Club was sponsoring it. Two of its members had volunteered to buy whatever supplies were necessary. The club was to reimburse them. They chose to buy their supplies at a store where one needed a store ID card in order to buy provisions.

After filling their cart with the needed supplies, they proceeded to the checkout counter and went through the line. The bill came to just over a hundred dollars. One of them had previously agreed to pay the bill with a personal check and be reimbursed by the Men's Club. It turned out that the store only accepted personal checks from the one whose name was on the membership card. The one with the stores ID card did not have his checkbook with him. Neither man had enough cash on them so they decided to leave without buying what they needed and shop where they would accept personal checks.

In amazement, the next person in line to checkout stepped forward, gave her store credit card to the cashier, and paid the bill. She said that she would be honored to pay our bill to help our church. In shock, both men stood there and couldn't think of a thing to say for a few moments. Still bewildered they thanked her and extended an invitation to join them on the day of the fish fry. The two men left the store with grateful hearts and with a lesson of how ANGELS UNAWARE play a part in our daily lives. This particular Angel did not attend the fish fry, but she will be remembered for her assistance in making it a successful event. Both men were left with the thought, "Did this just happen to us?"

The third incident is as follows;

This incident happened in Mississippi. Two men were fishing on Lake Arkabutla. Fishing was rather slow so they decided to call it a day and proceeded to leave the lake. When one of them was hooking the boat to the trailer, he all of sudden fell to the ground. In the next boat in line to leave the lake there was a woman who observed the fisherman falling and not moving. She immediately told those with her to take her to shore and to take care of the boat. With the help of the fisherman's friend she got the fallen fisherman into her car and she drove him to the hospital some thirty miles or so from the lake. It turned out to be that this woman was a trained paramedic and recognized a problem when she saw one. Was it a coincident that that paramedic was in the boat behind the person who needed help or was it an Angel in disguise? I choose to believe that that paramedic was an Angel in disguise.

These three incidents brings to light that there are Angels among us and that they are here to help when and where help is needed. God put each one of these Angels where they were needed most, for He directs the lives of those who commit their lives to His service.

A Write's Prayer

Guide my hands O Lord let them write whatever
You want me to say.

Let them glide across the paper and leave behind
Your thoughts for the day.

Mistakes I will make I know, forgive me Lord for
I only heard a part of what You had to say.

Help me clear my mind O Lord I pray, for it is
Your will I seek this day.

Yesterday went well for me O Lord because I
listened to what You had to say.

Today my mind is not so receptive O Lord, so I
am here to pray.

Tomorrow will be a new day, I will seek Your
will O Lord, I know that You will help
me along my way.

Hold me by the hand O Lord so that I may
walk by your side.

When in the puddles of sin I walk O Lord
help me keep my feet dry through
Thy word.

Hold Your hand over me like an umbrella
O Lord and may Your love wipe all
of my fears away.

Clothe me in Your grace O Lord so that I
might see the path You have for
me to trod.

Help me O Lord, for some days I know not
which way to go or what to say.

Guide my hand O Lord as I seek words
worthy of Thy name.

When at last I lay my pen down O Lord
take my hand as I pass from this
life and let me hear, "Welcome
my child, you are home
to stay".

A Shy Beginning

---⊶⊷⊶⊷---

I remember the days when I was a young lad and hid behind my mother's apron when friends came to call. As much as she tried, I would rather be seen and not heard.

These were the days that I preferred to call my dog (Snooky), run, and play in the woods or go to the shore and row my skiff or search along the shore in the seaweed to see what treasures I could find.

These were the years that I was too afraid to express myself for fear of being made fun of because I stuttered and had a problem of being around people. Those were the years my older brother seemed to take pleasure in mocking me or other ways of dominating me. Because of this we would fight at the drop of a hat, being bigger and older he would keep it up until I would run away in tears. In turn, I would run, hide, and felt more comfortable being alone.

I came to think that I was of little use to my family, friends or myself, so I continued to avoid making friends or playing with other boys or girls. I was very shy around the opposite sex and often avoided playing games where girls were involved. Though my two sisters would stick up for me my older brother would not leave me alone. I also have to admit that I goaded my brother in hopes of getting him in trouble, but for the most part, it was the other way around.

During my scouting years (Boy Scout and Sea Scout) I met Ed Proudfoot and for whatever reason we became friends and formed a friendship that lasted a lifetime. We hung around together during our school years, got into trouble together and had a bond that I should have had with my older brother. We joined the military service together, though we never served together. He became a radio operator and I became an airplane mechanic, we both served in the Army Air Corp. during WW11. After the war, we continued to be friends up until his death. I still consider his children as part of my own family.

After the war my brother and I drifted apart and went our separate ways, although we lived in the same town and interacted on occasions we never had the relationship that siblings normally have.

By now, my shyness had abated, but I was still bothered by a slight speech impediment and had to form my sentences carefully to avoid stuttering. In many ways, I am still a loner and enjoy the beauty, I find in the great outdoors.

When God called me to write I felt that I was not qualified to write, let alone for God. Over the years, I have come to express myself through my pen and have enjoyed every minute I spend putting on paper what He wants me to convey to others. Writing is the last profession that I would have chosen for myself. In school English was my worst subject, if I got a C on my report card I was pleased. I have found that one does not have to be properly schooled to fulfill their calling, for God will supply every need when one submits to His will. I know that as long as I live I will continue to write and express to others whatever God wants me to put on paper.

From being an introvert as a child to becoming, a published author has been a great journey, one with many difficulties. Anywhere from being shy to running my own business, serving in the military during the time of war, divorce, falling to the temptations of Satan, being saved through the intervention of Jesus Christ, being called to write (of which I knew nothing). Would I change anything? Looking back perhaps, I would change some things, but considering what I have been through and looking at it as a time of preparation for what God wanted me to do, no I would not change a thing, even as painful as some of them were.

I regret some things I did and wish others did not happen, but now I see them as a time of growth, both mentally and spiritually. Without these lessons of life and the intervention of Jesus Christ, I would still be wandering around in the darkness of life without the assurance of eternal life. God has taught me many lessons by allowing me to go through some of the hardest times in my life (with Him by my side) and for these times, I am very grateful, for they have brought me ever closer to Him.

A PHOTOGRAPH

A photograph is an image frozen
in time.

Expressions on the faces remain
the same.

A dog is suspended in that jump
for all time.

The smile upon that face, though
it was long ago will never
change.

A photo may yellow with time
but the subject is still
young, no matter
their age.

A glimpse of yesteryear with
the décor remaining
the same.

With a look on a face, the hair
style the same, nothing
will ever change.

Though our thoughts grow dim,
a photograph sparks them
anew, we recall the
old as though
it were
new.

Our mind is like a photo album
when we recall the old as
though it were new.

Flashbacks pass through our minds
as we grow old and wish we
could have them frozen
in time.

But old we must grow, just like the
yellow photos we have stored
in our mind.

Photos frozen in time are like our
memories of old, we cherish
them and bring them
to mind whenever
we take the
time.

A Mountain Stream

As the waters of the mountain stream cascade towards the sea, they bring life to the land all-around.

The cascading waters are like music in the ear of those who pause along a mountain stream and drink in the beauty that abounds.

The fisherman casts his lure into the clear deep pools trying to catch a trout for his evening meal.

As the day gives way to night, the fisherman builds a fire by the edge of the stream, there to spend the night.

During the darkness of the night he observes the heavens above and marvels at the sparkling stars all shinny and bright, then falls into a restful sleep.

Just before dawn he awakens to the call of a lonely wolf high up the mountain, stirs the fire and warms himself as the sun breaks the eastern sky.

A day and night by a mountain stream refreshes the soul, reminding us that God is in control, displaying the beauty of His hand to all who have eyes to see.

A Daughter's Memory Of
Her Parents Divorce

My Dad! That is how I have always felt; he was always the special sunshine in my childhood.

My earliest memories of those days were just feelings. I remember feeling that something was not right. I went shopping one day with my mother and on the way; she stopped and made a phone call from a phone booth. When she came back to the car, she was happy. I had no idea what it was she talked about or with whom she talked. I knew it was out of character, my uneasy feelings started then.

Once I remember two men coming to the house with two bicycles. Dad did not act as though they were very welcome and at the time, I thought that it must be that they were strangers. The adults, especially my parents were not comfortable with one another. One of the men was blind and I shied away from him. The bicycles were for my sister and me, but I did not want one of them. The blind man, he was different, he could even play cards. I have a vague recollection of an evening of playing cards around the kitchen table. That may have come later.

I felt sadness because my dad seemed unhappy. Then it happened one day, I answered the phone and a man asked for my mother. Dad grab the phone, he was very angry and told whomever it was to stop calling and to leave my mother and our family alone. I had never seen my dad angry before and it frightened me. I even think my mother was upset with my dad. I went for a long walk by myself, just to think.

I had heard of the word divorce, it was a bad word; it was the end of the world type of word. I cried and prayed that that was not happening. One day I found myself sitting on the hill overlooking the river, I had walked down a dirt road that ran behind our street so that no one could bother me and see that I was upset. I prayed so hard that God and my dad could make everything OK again, but something deep inside of my soul hurt and I knew that everything was about to change.

The next thing I remember dad was traveling, going here and there by himself. I wanted to make everything OK for him. Then he went to work in Connecticut and we went to see him for a weekend, we stayed in a motel and dad told my sister and me that we could share a bed. We could not stay where dad was living because he was staying in a room at a boarding house or something like that. All I cared about was that we were all together except for my younger brother; he had to stay at home with my Grandmother. Mom and dad were kind of nice to each other even though mom didn't seem that happy about the situation. I stuck to my dad; he was my hope to make everything all right again.

Dad came home for thanksgiving that year and I remember the turkey, it was going to be great. I do not know what started it, but then my parents started arguing and I knew for sure what was coming. We three kids were watching TV, dad came in very upset and angry, and he said that he had to leave because mom did not want him there anymore. My world came to a stop, my sister and brother cried and I thought that is was because I was crying. I knew that Peter did not understand what was going on and I was not sure whether Polly did or not.

All I could think was that this was wrong, mother was wrong. Someone had to take care of dad. I ran to my room, the window overlooked the driveway and I screamed to dad to take me with him. I had to take care of him. I hurt so badly because I thought that I would never see him again. My mother must be crazy! My dad was the best man in the world; someone pulled me from the window as I watched him drive away. We never did eat dinner that day and I cried a lot.

I knew that dad was close to his parents and we used to wait there for the school bus. Nana tried to explain that dad was OK and that we would see him, because my parents fought so much that that was why he left, so us kids would not be hurt. Hurt? Funny, I do not remember my parents ever arguing before this! Hurt was not strong enough for how I felt. Who would take care of dad? I prayed that God would look after him. Who would take care of dad's hurts? I told Nana that I wanted to be with dad so that I could take care of him. She said that he would be OK, she never said anything bad about mother, she just said that we would see dad.

I had to be strong and tough to help my brother and sister! Who was really going to take care of us now? Oh, mother was good to us; I do not remember talking to her much. I was angry with her because she made my dad go away. She had other interests.

Aunt Mabel spent a lot of time with us and she talked with us a lot. I remember dad coming once about seeing us kids. I was going to be thirteen and Polly's birthday was coming up. Dad wanted to take us for a weekend. At first mom said OK and then she said absolutely not, something frightened her and she thought that dad would not bring us back. That would not have bothered me! I asked Nana what was going on. She said that Peter was too young to go. Someone mentioned getting out of the state without problems, and then everything would be OK. Mom was trying to stop him because dad wanted to take us to New York City. Wow!!!, so much tension, then we were told we could go. What fun we had! I still have a little trinket from that trip in my jewelry box.

It is hard now to write about all of this. Sometimes I can see how much influence it has had on me as an adult. However as an adult when I realize what this time in my life did to me, I choose not to think about or understand it. For many years I blamed my mother for taking away an ideal childhood and trashing all of my happiness. I have looked everywhere to regain that and have finally begun to find the peace where it always was, within me.

Looking back before my parents' divorce, my childhood was very idealistic, I was happy, curious, and some of my memories stand out strong. Like fishnets being stretched out in the fields to dry before the winter snows came. Snow storms and dad seeming very important because he worked very long hours on the snowplows. Going scalloping in the fall of the year, up before dawn and on the water before the sun came up. With sunrise, all of the boats began their day's work of harvesting scallops, the smell of the ocean and the culling board still comes to mind. I loved the natural things and dad taught us so much. Once I dug some clay where the Indians used to live on the riverbanks at the end of our street. I made a small clay pot and let the sun bake it and then I painted it. I was proud; I had done it the Indian way. The winters were beautiful and I was the first one out in the morning after a fresh snowfall to see the quiet beauty of it before the other kids came out and knocked the snow from the tree branches. The summers were great! We helped Grandpa Phillips plant his gardens and worked in the fields (Phillips Farm, West Chatham). We also helped Grandma Nickerson at the Inn (Old Harbor Inn, North Chatham). I remember a few spankings from my mother, never from my dad. He was my hero, even when we had to mow the lawn, which was work. I was proud to show him that I could do what he had taught me.

All of these wonderful memories are just that, memories of perfection before my parents split up. Then he was gone, not forever, not very far. I missed running to him when he came home from work and giving him hugs. Now the hugs are fewer, but much more important.

A Barn Of Old

I once stood proud, my roofline was
straight and high.

My paint was new, my doors swung
easy, my windows were bright
and clean.

The horses and wagons under my
roof were kept warm and dry
while storms raged
outside.

The Darkies kept me clean and neat,
some labored from dawn till
night in the cotton fields
all around.

Never having much time for themselves
except on the Lord's Day when all
were required to listen to the
preacher as he prayed.

On Mondays all hands turned out to
start out the week anew.

Labor hard they did to fill the silos
with fodder to feed the cattle and
horses when cold was the
winter outside.

Hoping that it would last until spring
along with the hay that was
stored in my loft.

The children who were too young to
work the fields played in the
pond just outside.

Or caught a fish or two that would
make a meal for all to share.

Once in a while they played in the
hay, hoping not to be caught.

On the Lord's Day, I witnessed all
coming from far and near to
worship in the Chapel
just across the way.

Where one dueled for the hand of
his love and lost, he now
lies in peace under
the shade of
the trees.

I saw the would-be bride as she
stood by his grave in her
wedding gown of
white.

Mourning her loss as she would
never again, feel the press of
his lips against hers.

Sad days and happy days, I have
seen them all come and go.

Age has taken its toll on me just
as it has on you.

My ridge has sagged, my timbers
are weak and can no longer
hold my roof high.

Parts of me are now on the ground
and I can no longer hear
the voices of old.

No more children play or fish in the
pond or climb in my hay.

No more cattle can be heard from
within or the sounds of the
carriages as they came
and went.

My doors can no longer swing wide
as they now all hang askew,
rusted are their hinges
and broken too.

Holes in my roof that leak when it
rains, the wetness thereof
keeps me wet which
hastens my
decay.

Soon I will be just another pile of
rotted wood, where once I
stood tall and proud.

But O what a past I had and how
proud I was to shelter all who
came through my doors.

No longer do they come inside for
fear that a plank will break
and they will fall.

I do not want to hurt anyone so
please view me from afar.

I may be falling down and ready
to die but my memories are
still alive.

A Letter To Grandma
& Grampa Phillips

Dear Grandma and Grandpa,

As I sit at the foot of your grave, I recall the days when I was young and came to visit you where you lived on Kildee Hill in Harwich Port. You most always had sugar gingerbread or caraway-seed cookies and milk for me. I can still see you mixing the sugar gingerbread and the cookies and putting them in the oven of your cast-iron cook stove. I can still smell them and could not wait for them to finish cooking so that I could have some, along with a glass of milk. You even let me lick out the bowl and spoon you used to mix them.

I also recall your black iron sink with a deep well pump at one end that you used for your water supply. You let me work the pump handle so that I could get a cold glass of water. I used to ask for a drink of water so that I could work the pump. You had a lilac bush just outside of your kitchen window. The kitchen's sink drain went through the side of the house into a V-shaped wooden trough that emptied on the ground in the lilac bush. How tall it grew and how full of blossoms it was in the spring, its fragrance still lingers in my mind. I would pick a bouquet and take them

28

home with me to give to my mother. They were also picked and placed on the graves of loved ones on Memorial Day.

You had such a beautiful Rock Garden with a rose-arbor and a path winding through it and a bench to sit on to enjoy the flowers. I still have a picture of you and Grandpa sitting on that bench. Never a weed do I recall, but I do recall the white iron rabbit with pink eyes you had sitting among the Old Maid Pinks, the Hens and Chickens, the Hollyhocks, Roses and all of the rest of the flowers you loved so well. I also recall the birdbath you had in the middle of your circular driveway with bushes around it and watching the birds as they took a bath in its water. I still have that white bunny with pink eyes and would not part with it, I will hand it down to one of my children.

In the summertime you kept drinking water in a clay crock in your pantry, it was always nice and cool, it used to sweat and feel cool to the touch. How cool and refreshing it was when it was hot outside. The cellar stairs were also in the pantry. I remember the cellar as being round, made of bricks with a brick shelf all around it where you stored your canned fruits and vegetables. It had a small window in the foundation to let enough light in so that you see what you were looking for.

Over the cellar way were stairs that went to the second floor of the house where I slept whenever I stayed overnight. I recall staying over one night when I was around three years old and waking up during the night and cried for my mother. I cried so hard that you had to call my mother to come and get me. As I remember I was frightened by the car lights as they shone through the window as they passed by your house and made strange figures on the attic roof or made Grandpa' easel look like a person standing in the dark. I still remember the different figures in the roof boards that were created by the knots, cracks and water stains that were in the boards of the open roof. One I recall was like a pond with the figure of a man standing on one side of it and a bird or something like a bird floating in the water. The shingle nails that protruded through the roof boards with little splinters of wood protruding around them, which formed arms and legs, formed some other strange figures. In my imagination, I would see all kinds of figures and things when the car lights at night would shine across the roof boards.

In the living room, you and Grandpa had a radio and after dark, we listened to the different comedian programs. The radio used to fade in and out and make all kinds of strange noises and we would strain our ears to hear what was being said. You had that same radio during World War ll and I can still hear Edward R. Merrill reporting from London England telling about the bombings and the war news.

In the parlor, you had a pump organ that on occasions you allowed us kids to pump the organ that would make squeaky sounds as the organ ran out of air. The parlor was for special events, such as when you entertained guests or had a death in the family, other than that it was kept closed.

I can still see Grandpa' paintings hanging in different rooms of the house. There were two that I liked the most, one was of a lake on a moonlit night with a big tree leaning over the water with a full moon in the background, it had a rowboat tied to the tree, and it had a sandy beach area in the foreground. The other was of the earth as seen from outer space. If it were compared to a photograph taken by an astronaut of today, they would look very much alike. Grandpa did the most of his paintings in the late twenties and thirties. When he died in nineteen forty nine each grandchild received one of his paintings, mine was a painting of the rocky coast of Maine. It has waves breaking on the shore with a high dark rocky coast in the background. With the light just right, you can see the reflection of the moon on the clouds.

We all loved to hear you tell stories of when you went to sea with your father and mother. He was a sea Captain and sailed to the Orient and up and down the eastern seaboard in his later years. Of how your brother Sanford was born in Hong Kong China aboard your father's vessel and they hired a Chinese to care for him on the return trip home. Of how you were caught in a hurricane off the South Carolina coast and almost lost your ship and died because of the storm. Of how in later years your brother Sanford was in a ship wrecked off the North African coast. After making it to shore he and one other survivor were captured by Arabs and carried off into the desert and finally escaped and made their way to a seaport where they got passage to South America and two years later made it back home. Grandma, you certainly had an exciting and interesting life when you were young. (This and other sea stories are elsewhere in my writings.)

Aunt Emily and Uncle Earl along with their three boys, Forest, David and Philip lived with you and Grandpa while they built their new house. All of us boys would run and play in the woods out back of your house. We chewed dried oak leaves pretending that they were tobacco. We thought that we were pretty big and chewed because we wanted to chew just Grandpa did. We jumped off the top of a sandbank just to see how far down the sandbank we could jump. We dug tunnels in the sandbank and hid from one another. The day when one of the tunnels collapsed and almost buried us was the last time we did that. Then we used to climb the apple trees down the hill behind your house and eat green apples until we had a stomachache. Onetime Grandpa told us that we could catch the pigeons if we could put salt on their tails, so of to the house we would go to get salt. Grandma, you scolded Grandpa for telling us such things but after a while, you gave us some salt and off we went chasing pigeons. I can still see Grandpa chuckling to himself as he watched us in pursuit of the pigeons.

When Howard Johnson opened their ice cream shop just below your house on the corner of route twenty-eight and Sisson Road, we were all delighted, for to us that meant that we could go down the hill and get some ice cream whenever we visited you. It did not always work out that way but when it did, we sure enjoyed it. At that time, my favorite ice cream was Pistachio, I had a problem of pronouncing certain words and that was one of them. I stuttered and had a hard time getting the word out. The server would finally figure out what I was trying to say.

I remember your long hair and how you used to braid it into one long braid that went halfway down your back when you went to bed at night. In the morning, you brushed it out and sometimes you put it in a bun on the back of your head, but most of the time you pulled it together on the back of your head and held it with a rubber band.

Of how when you fixed Grandpa's meals you had to strain all of his food because he had stomach problems and could not eat his food unless it was strained. He told us that he chewed his food at least twenty one times before he swallowed it. Grandpa did have stomach problems but he also told us that he chewed tobacco since he was twelve years old. At Christmas time and on his birthday we gave Grandpa plug tobacco as a gift and he told us that plug tobacco was sweeter than candy. He always had a spit can beside his chair and most of the time there was a little on the floor.

How we loved to watch, Grandpa when he was making his windmills, listening to and watching the one-lunger engine run just outside of his wood working shop. It had a drive belt that went through the side of the shop, which drove a long shaft that had several drive belts off of it that drove his different machines. The smell of the fresh cut wood and even the smell of his spittoon as I passed by it still lingers. It was exciting as a child to watch him work. I remember you doing the most of the painting and then you displayed them in your front yard and on both sides of your driveway. To me it was quite a sight to watch all of the mills turning when the wind blew. The man sawing the log in two, the wooden maid watering her flowers, wooden sailboats, pots of wooden flowers, wooden weathervanes in the form of fish or a boat and all of the rest of his handiwork. It was fun to walk among them and pretend that I was doing the same thing that they were doing. The joys of being around you and Grandpa were endless and at the same time if I need to be reprimanded, you both did so with love.

Grandpa told us of the time he went fishing on the Grand Banks off the coast of Newfoundland, of how he vowed never to go again as it was no life for him. He told of dory fishing and the long hard hours they spent day after day with little or no rest for days on end. He told us of how one occasion when the cook and one of the seamen got into a fight and the cook chased the seaman around the galley with a big knife until finally the Captain broke it up before someone got hurt. One reason he never went again he told us was that once at sea they never saw land again until they had their hold full of fish and that could take from two to three months, depending on how plentiful the fish were.

One of his favorite stories was about a man who was walking home at dusk and decided to take a short cut through the woods. He came to a swamp and decided that he would go through the swamp instead of going around it when he heard a tree toad and a bullfrogs having a conversation. He heard the tree toad call out in shrill voice, "Knee deep, knee deep" and the bullfrog replied in a low deep voice, "Better go round, better go round." Then he would chuckle and smile as only he could. He enjoyed telling that story as much as we enjoyed hearing it.

Grandpa told us that he had invented a way of getting water out of a well by the use of high-pressure air. He claimed that one could release high-pressure air below the water line in the well and that the air would force the water to the top of the well and that it would overflow from the well and then be pumped into a storage tank for future use. Grandpa had a good mechanical mind and often spent time trying to figure out how to improve how things were done.

He had a sheep dog with long hair by the name of Sally; she was white with black marking. He had her well trained and she would do whatever he told her to do, like rolling over and playing dead, jumping over his cane, sitting up and begging, along with other tricks. I can still see Grandpa sitting in his rocking chair in his woodworking shop with Sally lying on the floor beside him.

Grandma, the memories of you coming to me when I lived in St. Louis, Mo. thirty four years after your death is without a doubt one of the highlights of my life. Much of it is still a mystery to me but I know that one day I will fully understand how and why it happened. For now, I believe that it was your way of letting me know that you were all right and that when we leave this existence we do not take any of our problems or health issues with us. It also showed me that the diseases of the body do not go with us when we leave this life. You had cancer when you died and weighted around seventy-five pounds, when you came to me you were as you were before you had cancer. Proof that when we die we put on a new body; one prepared for us by our Lord and Savior, Jesus Christ. Grandma, you answered many questions for me about life and death, at the same time a lot more questions came to mind.

I know that you are now free from all your earthly problems and are at rest in the arms of our Lord and Master, Jesus Christ. You set a good example for all who knew you. Thank you Grandma for the love and care that you showered upon us when we were young. No one could have set a better example for us to follow and you were truly an inspiration for all who knew you.

Your loving Grandson
Merrill Phillips

P. S. I pray that I can be an inspiration to others as you were when I was young. I know that I have some very big shoes to fill in order to follow your example, not only in life but in death also. You showed me that I do not have to know all of the answers now, they will come soon enough.

A SALUTE TO THE FALLEN

Johnny stopped by today O Lord, he
wanted to say goodbye, he was
on his way to his heavenly
home.

He gave his all on the field of battle
Lord, he gave his life to keep
the rest of us free.

Oh, how he loved his wife and family,
he knew no other way, but to
fight for those he loved.

On the day, he died Lord he told me
to tell his family goodbye.

Johnny is on his way home Lord, he
stopped by to say goodbye.

He was at peace Lord, the day that he
died, he never shed a tear or
blinked an eye.

The sting of death took the gleam out of
his eyes Lord, he also said that he
loved you O Lord and was
ready to die.

He left this world a better place O Lord,
he was a friend to all he met,
especially the children he
befriended while
waging war.

Johnny shared his love for life with all
O Lord, even those on the
other side.

He went without some days so that he
could share his food with the
children as they romped
and played.

He was a good man O lord, his love for
country and family came from
deep inside.

Johnny made a difference in this cruel
old world O Lord, with a smile on
his face he closed his eyes in
death and said, "Goodbye".

Family and friends will miss him O
Lord, but the memories he left
behind will sustain them
when they bring his
name to mind.

There are many Johnny's who will not
come home from the battlefields
of the world, thank their
families for keeping
you free.

A Tribute To Grandma Phillips

My heart is full of joy whenever I think of you.
my soul rejoices as your words ring true.

You are now with Jesus Grandma,
for my heart tells me it is true.

Your words of love ring in my ears as I
remember the days of old.

I still feel your tender touch as though you were
still holding me close to you.

I miss you Grandma and wish that you were still here,
however, I know that you are at peace and rest in
the arms of Jesus.

Thoughts of you bring back memories of old. The sugar
gingerbread and milk sitting on your kitchen table
in anticipation of my arrival.

Eating too many green apples in the fall of the year
and the bellyaches that went along with them.

I remember you scolding Grandpa for telling us that we
could catch the pigeons by putting salt
on their tails.

With a smile on his face, we chased them from place
to place, never quite achieving our goal. We
laughed and giggled as we tried.

I still see you Grandma standing in your doorway
waving goodbye as we left for home.

But most of all I miss the love you showed towards me,
your kind words and hardly ever a scold, makes
my memories of you ever more pleasant.

CHILDHOOD MEMORIES

Once my father told me in a telephone conversation that I had been a better son to him than he had been a father to me. I do wish that he had spent more time with me as a child, but he was so busy making a living that he had little time to spend with us five children. He farmed during the summer months and either went fishing or worked as a carpenter during the winter months. During WW II, he worked at Camp Edwards or another Army Camp in Virginia during the winters. All of these jobs required him to be up early in the morning and he never got home until way after dark. We were too young to comprehend that the country had been through a depression and that we were poor. We always had a place to live, food on the table and clothes to wear; this was due to the sacrifices that my father made so that his family might have the essentials of life. We did do things with him, but most of the time it was on a work basis, from cutting firewood to working in the fields, weeding in the garden, or cutting and storing hay for the upcoming winter. The biggest part of our childhood was work related.

Occasionally my older brother and I did get to go hunting with him. I remember the time he took me with him hunting for geese. It was wintertime and the salt ice was piled high on the shore. We sat on the ice with white sheets over us so that the geese could not see us, before going home; he let me shoot his gun. We got both some geese and ducks that day that made a meal for the whole family. Hunting was one of dad's pleasures in life; it gave him a chance to do something that he enjoyed as well as proving food for his family.

During the trapping season, he trapped muskrat, skunk, fox and whatever else was available. He worked at whatever he had to, to make a living. He was not one to sit around the house and complain that there was not anything to do.; he always found some way to make a dollar. When the PWA program was in force, he worked for fifty cents an hour to provide for his family.

When father started farming he did so with horses and horse drawn equipment. I still remember driving the horse while father handled the horse drawn equipment. Before planting he hand marked the rows and it was my brothers and my job to help him plant the different kinds of seed. While doing this my brother and I planted each other's name in the rows with the seeds and when they came up, we heard about it from father. Father loved farming and had a close relationship and respect for the soil; he had a green thumb and could raise most everything without much difficulty. In the spring when the herring was running, he caught them by the truckload and used them as fertilizer. As boys, we took the row from the herring and sold them to our friends and neighbors to make spending money. Father worked the fields from sunrise until dark, looking back on it, I now realize how much father loved what he was doing and that he loved his family very much, although he was not one to express his love openly.

When it came to where he could afford it, he made himself a homemade tractor instead of buying one. He took an old dump truck, stripped it down to its frame, and re-worked it. He put a four-speed transmission behind a three-speed transmission and a re-built six-cylinder engine, I remember helping to grind in the intake and exhaust valves and putting the engine back together. When both transmissions were in low gear, one had to take a mark on the tractor to see if it was moving. He used this tractor for years until he could afford to buy a factory built one.

After many years of farming, he installed an irrigation system and no longer did he have to depend upon the rain to water the farm. This was when the farm became profitable. He had a roadside stand where he sold his produce to the public. It was twenty feet square with a drop down front. When he finally sold the farm, he had a store one hundred feet in length and forty feet in depth. Father preferred to build whatever he needed instead of hiring it done. Instead of buying the bed-stock for the farm, he started them from seed in the window of his house and when the weather warmed in the spring, he moved them to a homemade hothouse until it became planting time.

Father was a quiet man and never had too much to say and was very slow to anger. I recall only once when father got angry and that was when someone took my brother's hunting license away from him, just because this person heard someone shoot after hunting hours and thought that it was he who was doing the shooting. He happened to be one of the town selectman and was a rather arrogant person. When father heard about it, he went to the selectman's house and demanded his son's license back. Upon refusing to return the license, the selectman called the police. The chief of police was my father's uncle and upon his arrival at the selectman's home, he got father calmed down and got my brother's license back. When father did get angry, for whatever the reason, no one had better get in his way and at the same time if he was wrong he would admit it. He was not a big man in stature, but he was wiry and had the strength of a much larger person. He would walk away from an argument rather than provoke one. I never knew of him physically hurting anyone, but if provoked enough I am sure he was more than capable of defending himself. He was well liked by all who knew him and not one to cheat anyone out of anything.

The time that he wanted a boat to go scalloping in, he bought an old Cat Boat, re-built it, and put an engine in it. It turned out to be one of the most seaworthy boats around. He would go scalloping in weather when most of the boats did not leave their moorings. I remember one day when I went with him, it was a windy, nasty day, but scalloping was good that year and we went anyway. While getting to the fish grounds we had whitewater over top of us most of the way, we were one of two boats that went that day. It was the roughest day that I had ever been scalloping and on the way, the engine quit and father had to go below deck and get the engine started again. In the meantime, we were bobbing around like a cock-stopple in a gale of wind, but the old boat lived up to her name "Catboat". She had nine lives and this was not her time to go.

Like most of the men of my hometown, Chatham, Mass., father had a great love for the sea and at the same time, he had a great respect for it. Many men from Chatham have lost their lives while fishing, men who knew the perils of the sea and just how quickly the sea can take a life. He had a narrow escape one day while fishing close to land. The engine quit and by the time he got it going again the boat was almost in the surf where if caught in the surf both boat and those on it were in danger of being lost.

My Uncle Horace (Horace's wife was my father's sister) had a wood, coal and oil business and some winter's father would cut wood for him. He and another man would go into the woods and fell trees all day long, chop, split and stack a cord of wood a day with axes. I use to go with them occasionally, it was back breaking work, but looking back on it, it was a good life, being out of doors and living close to nature. It was a simple life and in its own way, it had its rewards. All part of living in the days of the Great Depression.

Seldom did father attend church, but had to have had a close relationship with God in his own way, for no one could love the soil and the outdoors like he did and not have a great reverence for the one who created it. Farming, commercial fishing and carpentry was his life. One of the few trips that he ever took was with our Uncle Roy. They packed their provisions into a boat, sailed to Monomoy Point, and camped on the beach for a week. They dug their own waterhole and lived off whatever they could find, such as fish, shellfish and the like. They also took a crystal radio that they had built themselves along with a battery to operate it.

It was not until a few years before father retired that he and mother went to Florida for the winters. Where they eventually bought a mobile home and spent their last years living in Chatham during the summer and in Florida during the winter. They both deserved this quiet time in their lives. If they ever had any differences, they never let it show in front of us children. Like any other married couples, they must have had problems, but nothing that they did not settle between them.

At retirement, my father sold the farm to my older brother who ran it for many years before he sold it to a developer who turned it into a subdivision. My brother kept the store and sold it to someone who tore the old store down and built a new one and is now known as "The Corn Patch." A piece of the past lost forever in the name of progress.

Mother died in Florida in 1977, father died in 1981. The farm known as "Phillips Farm" consisted of eight acres of land in West Chatham, Cape Cod, Mass. Father purchased the farm in 1929, which consisted of sixteen acres. His sister Rachel and her husband, Horace Bearse, owned the lower half that abuts Oyster River.

CHRISTMAS SEASON

May the Lord's blessings fall upon you and your
family as gentle rain and nourish your soul.

May He sustain you as you spread His word
among the lost souls of this world.

When facing adversity look to God for the strength
to step out in faith and follow your calling.

This is the time of year to celebrate the birth of our
Lord Jesus Christ, who came to earth to live
among His created beings.

A time of a new beginning for those you have touched over
the years, like new born babes may they grow to be strong
in faith as they feed upon God's word.

The Christmas season is truly a time of renewal and
a time to come to the stable of innocence
and renew your vow of service to the
King of kings and Lord of lords.

Hold your lamp of God's word high; be as a "Light"
set upon a hill, a "Light" to all who are
struggling to change their lives, one
that will bring them closer to
living a more Christ
like life.

When discouraged turn to God in prayer and He in
turn will open a new door, step through that door
with a grateful heart for what he has done for
you in the past and use those experiences
to encourage others to fulfill their
calling as you have fulfilled
yours.

A Boy's Best Friend

———∽⋙⋘∞———

Come on Snooky, come and play with me, we will
run and chase across the fields and
through the woods.

When you get through chasing the rabbits, follow
my scent to wherever I might be.

Remember when we went to the river, I rowed
my boat and you chased me along
the shore?

You would jump a rabbit and chase it for a while,
then back to the river you would come to
see if I was still there.

We would chase and play in the swamps all the
day long, when thirsty we drank from the
spring when the tide was low.

When at the end of the day we went home, we both
collapsed and slept the whole night through.

Those were the days when all we had to do was to
run and play, you chased the rabbits while I
dug clams and a bond between us grew.

Under the warmth of the old kitchen stove you
birthed your puppies and shared them
with those, you loved.

Times when you came home smelling like a skunk,
trying to share the smell with us all, then off
to the barn you went until the smell
went away.

Or I would wash you in tomato juice in hopes of
making you smell nice and clean.

Sometimes I came home with that awful smell, then
I too was marched off to the barn, where mother
stripped me down and washed me with
tomato juice and lye soap before I
was allowed back into
the house.

We would run and chase as free as young fawns and
do the things a young boy and his dog
would do.

Then came the day when you were no longer there, I
was told you had gone where all good dogs go.

After that when I went to the river I would sit on the
bank and listen for your bark when you
used to chase the rabbits.

However, the only sounds that I could hear were those
in my mind as you ran far and near.

You were a boy's best friend Snooky, and will always be
a part of me.

ARTIST

Sometimes I feel like an artist, one who uses word to paint a picture in the minds of those who read my works.

Words used to draw a picture that so impresses one's heart that they want to share that picture with others.

It is only through the Holy Spirit that I have had some success in that regard, for the words that I select are not of my own, but selected by the comforter that Jesus promised before He ascended into heaven, the Holy Spirit or sometimes called the Holy Ghost.

As time has passed, I have come to depend on that still small voice that awakens me during the dark of the night and urges me to put pen to paper and record what He wants me to say.

Not always have I been obedient, thus losing opportunities to paint a portrait with words for someone to ponder.

Whether during the dark of the night or the bright of day, it is and has been an honor and privilege to put on paper whatever the Holy Spirit urges me to say.

Sometimes it is a special piece for a dear friend, intended to help them cope with a trial in their life, other times it is to comfort and show God's love towards all of us.

Whether short or long every endeavor brings me closer to God, they fulfill my desire to have a positive influence on the lives I touch.

For what I have received I thank God and praise His Holy name whenever I hear someone say, "Your writings have helped me."

I too have benefited from my own endeavors, they have brought me closer to God and I have come to realize that God has prepared me for this task the most of my life by allowing me to go through trials where I had to depended upon Him to see me through.

He has trusted me and encouraged me to be a part of His plan for the advancement of His kingdom here on earth. I do not say this as boasting, I say it in all humility. I never thought that I would ever be good enough to take such a part, no, not in my wildest dreams, but now that I am I will do my best to live up to what I have been called to do. If I ever receive any accolades for my works, I will direct them to where they belong, before the throne of God, for without Him I am as nothing.

From High Above

———⊶⊷———

There is no greater place to relax than in a seat of a jumbo jet, looking out of a window at thirty nine thousand feet, flying at near six hundred miles an hour.

The clouds below are like a vast field of snow with the sun reflecting off of its surface, off in the distance can be seen the contrail of another jet racing towards its destination, such as we.

A delightful breakfast served by our stewardess made the flight even more enjoyable for those fortunate enough to have a first class seat on this giant of the skies.

The cloud formations change as we race across the skies at breakneck speed, an occasional opening in the clouds reveal the earth far below, super highways appear to be nothing but a pencil mark on a page.

Off in the distance can be seen clouds that appear as erupting volcanoes, forming many different shapes, never two the same, beauty not seen from below.

The plane serves as a platform from which to observe the cities and farmland far below, the rivers look more like slithering snakes as they make their way through the hills and mountains as they meander their way towards the sea.

Over the mountainous regions, the sun reflects off the pristine waters of the lakes as they pass in review, of all sizes and shapes these lakes hold the waters that supplies life to the cities and forests that dot the landscape far below.

Cities and towns nestle along the banks of the rivers with roads dispersing in all directions, some to the mountains where the ski slopes twist and turn as they make their way to the ski lodges and the warmth of a cozy fire, others cross the mountains to the cities and towns on the other side.

The trucks and cars appear as toys as they too speed their way across this great land we call America, they are as so a child could pick one up and play with it until tiring and letting it go.

From this great height one can certainly get a different perspective of this blue planet that God hung in its place so long ago, a marvel to those who believe that God created this planet just for you and me, a place we can call home, without God and this blue planet where would we be?

Behold from such a great height we too for a fleeting moment can imagine what earth looks like from God's perspective, not in the same light but certainly in a light not seen from the ground.

Everything looks so tranquil from this perch in the sky, it is almost impossible to see the turmoil that exists so far below, if only the leaders of all nations could meet this high above the world turmoil, surly they could ease or even bring to an end the wars and hatred that now exists thirty nine thousand feet below.

The plane begins to slow, indicating that it is time to leave our lofty perch and return to the earth far below, a restful and tranquil flight it has been, a time to reflect on that which is far more important than just living life to please ourselves, from on high we can get a better view of this great land we call home.

The lower we get the more we realize how fast and far we have traveled in such a short period of time, for from Chicago to Boston is just over a two hour flight.

Lower and lower we go, approaching the runway at what seems like breakneck speed, over the waters of Boston Harbor we skim, ships and boats, all headed in different directions pass in review.

As the plane touches the runway it lurches as its wheels touch the runway, then the nose wheel joins the man landing gear as the captain of this ship of the air reverses the thrust of the jet engines as we slow to a reasonable speed, a mere fraction of the speed we were traveling an hour ago.

Taxiing from the runway to the gate of departure seems slow indeed, for this great plane is built for speed, not just a few miles an hour as when we approach the gate and finally come to a stop, what a way to travel in an age such as ours.

All becomes quiet as the jet engines become silent, their job well done and quiet they will remain until another crew takes over and brings them to life again and starts a new trip to wherever it is destined to go.

GONE ARE THE DAYS

As I walk across the clam-flats towards the open sea,
the clams reveal their hiding place by the
shower of water they squirt into
the air as I pass by.

As I stand before the breaking seas they lap upon my
feet, I gaze far at sea, searching for a sail
of yesteryear.

The smell of the salt air gives me a high, bringing back
memories of sailing the seven seas in search
of treasures beyond my dreams.

Seagulls soaring just above the rolling seas dip and dive
as they catch their next meal.

An oil slick from a school of fish just beyond the breaking
surf reveal their location to a lonely fisherman
as he casts his lure towards the same.

Chilly air comes from a fogbank just off of the shore and
cools the fevered brow.

Sounds of a foghorn can be heard from afar, as it warns
passing ships to be beware of dangers ahead.

In the fall of the year when I wandered the beach I stopped
and rubbed some bayberries between my fingers and
smelt their fragrant upon my hands.

Picking as any as I could find I took them home and extracted
their wax and made candles to light the dark of
the winter nights to come.

Coming across wild cranberries, I picked all I could and made
savory sauce to be served during the holidays ahead.

With the snows and the winter ice came
the arctic geese, searching
the shoals for their daily needs.

I in turn hid under a white sheet, hoping to shoot a plump goose
to go along with a duck or two for the upcoming
holiday meal.

To open a camp door during the winter and see a weasel in his
white winter coat scurrying for the shelter of the
sand dunes outside.

To witness a fox chasing a rabbit on a moonlit night is a sight
to behold, running out of sight the rabbit ran for its
life to stay alive.

Overhead on a dark night the stars danced brightly, wondering
where they came from and what kept them from falling
on my head filled my mind.

Laying on the beach at night, staring
into the heavens, wondering
when, why, and who put such beauty up there for us
to enjoy?

In the pre-dawn hours to be awaken
by the sound of gentle waves
breaking upon the shore, then arise and watch in
wonderment as the sun rose from the
depths of the sea.

Creating a ribbon of fire from the horizon to the shore, surly a
picture painted by the hand of God for man's delight.

Other times sitting by the edge of the sea watching ships of sail
heading for foreign lands, stirring the sense of
adventure within.

Wondering where they were going and
what treasures they carried
in their holds, watching the decks hands as they went
about their chores as they passed from sight.

Wondering how far at sea they would be
by night or if they would be
in a safe port when the gales blow?

Remembering of how we lived in a
fisherman's shanty by the edge of
the sea during the warm summer months and romped and
played in the tide pools with the small sea creatures,
caught there between the tides.

Never to wear a pair of shoes from June
until it was time to go back
to school, to run and play all day by the ocean's edge served
to build memories for when we became old to tell
our grandchildren of how you were raised.

Today the young can no longer run and play by the ocean's edge
as they did when I was young, for all of the public lands
no longer exist; they are now under the domain
of the government and all access is
limited to guided tours.

The days of wandering the beaches are gone and gone too are the
sails of old.

Today, the life of the days of sail and
roaming the beaches are only
spun in tales such as this, the children of today will never
know the adventures and games we played by the
ocean's edge, for they no longer exist.

Letting Go

Through the resent death of my twin sister (Mary Emma Phillips, Nickerson) I have come to know that there is a time of letting go and allowing a loved one to die in dignity and in the presence of loved ones.

At the time of Mary's death I was spending the evening with my son and his family and was spared the ordeal of watching my sister take her last breath and go on to a new existence.

I am sorry that I was not there, but at the same time, I know that it would have been a most trying time to see someone you love take their last breath and not be able to do anything about it.

Her medical problems were many. For almost thirty years she was a diabetic, she was a cancer patient, her pancreas was failing, her liver was shutting down, one of her lungs had failed, she needed bypass surgery, and through an agreement with the doctor, she was put on live support, which was against her living will.

Even through all of these problems Mary was coherent right up to a day and a half before she died, she was a strong person and fought for life until death finally overwhelmed her.

Mary knew before the rest of us that she would never leave her hospital bed alive and she came to terms with it and settled all of her earthly problems before closing her eyes in death.

During her lifetime, Mary had many problems with personal relationships, both in the family and outside of the family. She lived as a recluse and spent many lonely years after her husband's death.

It was not until she was on her deathbed that she faced these problems and reconciled them. She herself said, "I cannot lie here on my death bed with these things on my mind" and asked forgiveness of those who she had offended and more importantly she asked forgiveness from God for her acts of sin.

Through her son Wayne she reaffirmed her faith and trust in Jesus Christ and put all of her trust in God to see her through her final act of life.

With her three sons, David, Wayne, and Ralph, Wayne's wife, Joyce, Ralph's wife, Marty, her grandson David Jr. and his wife by her side the doctors removed all life support and in her final act of life Mary picked her head up off of her pillow and looking around her room twice and looked each and everyone in their eyes with peace on her face and then laid her head back on her pillow and took her last breath.

Perhaps Mary could have lived a while longer on life-support, but to me she was suffering too much (even though she was well medicated) not to let her go.

I was asked by her family to conduct the graveside services and with much humility, I felt honored to do so. She was buried by her husband's side and remained faithful to him even unto death.

We all have a time to be born and a time to die and no matter what procedures the medical profession may take, they cannot change either one, for this is directly under the control of God.

All involved should rejoice that we had Mary with us for so many years (74 years), for at the time of her birth she was not supposed to live. The attending doctor did all he could to get her to breathe, but to no avail. Through the efforts of our grandmother, Mary took her first breath.

By dunking Mary first in a tub of cold water and then in a tub of hot water grandmother was able to shock Mary into taking her first breath. She then placed Mary in a shoebox lined with cotton in front of an open oven door for warmth.

Today if Mary had the choice of being in heaven or returning to earth, I have no doubt that Mary would choose to stay in heaven, free from all sin, disease, and suffering.

I miss my twin sister and hold many good memories of our lives together, but I know there comes a time when we must let go of those we love and allow them to live and die under our great conductor of life, God.

My Walk With God

I regret not the trials of life I have had to endure; they have brought me closer to my Lord and Savior, Jesus Christ.

The miles I have walked have not wearied my feet; rather they have taken me to places where God wanted me to go.

By night, I rest under the heavenly skies and watch the stars dance high over my head and give thanks to God for the blessings He has bestowed upon me.

Awakening just before the break of day I watch as God paints a new painting in the eastern sky as the sun begins its journey across the sky.

Each sunrise gives me the inspiration to rise from my night's sleep and continue my journey of life.

O, how sweet it is to cleanse my body in the falling rain, rain that You send to nourish the fruit of the earth.

From my youth to my days of old I have endeavored to walk the path that You have laid out before me.

Not always have I been true to Thee, but at those times, I bent my knees before Thy throne and sought forgiveness of my trespasses.

Being the forgiving God that You are You remember them no more and encourage me to forgive those who have offended me.

When I live life my way You do not abandon me to my own devices, rather You open the doors that bring me back to Thee.

With open arms, You welcome me back to Thy fold and wash me clean as the newly fallen snow with the blood that You shed while hanging on the cross of Calvary.

I know my days here on Earth will one-day end, I fear not that day for You have promised me a new life, a life free from the sins that now entice me to stray.

What a day that will be, my soul will rejoice as it soars into the heavenly realm and I hear You say, "Welcome my child, come and receive your reward for being faithful till the end."

Old Glory

---◇◇◇◇---

O, what a sight to see; Old Glory un-furling in an early morning breeze, her stars and stripes tattered and torn from the shellfire that filled the night sky.

The night had been long, the night had hidden the death of battle, and flares at times lit up the darkened sky revealing the advancing troops as they lay down a barrage of death.

On they came, hell bent on annihilating those who were fighting for freedom, the freedom to live a peaceful life and one devoted to the causes of Christianity.

During the height of battle as the shells burst in air, they could catch a glimpse of Old Glory and this gave them the courage to withstand the onslaught of the heathen army as it advanced towards their position.

The cry of the wounded was all around, but Old Glory never came down, not during that night or any other night was anyone willing to give in and allow Old Glory to fall to the ground.

Old Glory has flown over the battlefields of the world for the cause of freedom and when the battles were over those who had fought gallantly gathered around Old Glory and in prayer thanked their heavenly Father for keeping them safe and free.

The next time you see Old Glory flying proudly over the land of the free remember those who gave their life so that the rest of us could remain free, they gave their all for freedom and the privilege of living in a nation where Old Glory is the flag of the free and the brave.

Old Glory is more than a flag; she represents a nation that is willing to defend herself from all aggression, whether it is at home or some foreign land.

The resolve to be free and remain free has been tried over and over again, from here to Tripoli Old Glory has flown over mighty fleets to the Doughboys of Flanders Field and never has she gone down in defeat.

At times we have lost battles where Old Glory was torn from her perch on high and desecrated, only to be raised in victory at the end of the war, God has blessed this great nation and always will as long as we the people stand up for freedom and bow our heads before the throne of God.

Each star and every stripe is the pride of our nation and as long as our fighting men and women stand behind her and hold her high Old Glory will always fly over the land of the free and the brave, the land we call America.

MOM

When I was a newborn, I lay in the protection of my mother's arms.

She nourished me and cared for me and supplied my every need.

She rocked me to sleep and then gently lay me in my bed and watched over me all the nightlong.

When I was sick she sat by my bed and held my hand and cooled my fevered brow.

As I grew, she sheltered me from the cruel of the world until I was old enough to hold my own.

When I came home with a bloody nose or scraped knee, she consoled me and wiped my tears away.

During my early school years, she awakened me and brushed me up all nice and clean.

Every Sunday she made sure I went to Sunday School to learn about the Lord from the time I was old enough until I was way up in school.

She defended me when the bullies tried to push me around.

She seemed to always know when I was in need and what to do to calm me down.

Just a kiss on the cheek or a hug usually made things better and took the hurt away.

My mother went without so that I could have things that we could not afford.

All through my school years, she saw to it that I had what I needed so that I could stay in school.

Then came the war years and my turn to leave home to defend my country.

Mother shed many a silent tear and prayed for my brother and me while we were helping to keep our country free.

She never gave in when the times were hard, she just buckled down and never complained.

When my brother and I came home from serving our country she cried once more, but this time they were tears of joy, because her sons had returned home.

Even after marriage mom was always there when I needed a shoulder to cry on.

She never interfered in affairs not her own. She prayed a lot and encouraged me to do the same.

On her deathbed we all gathered around to let her know that we loved her and held her hand.

Even in dying, she never complained. She just laid there and took things as they came.

Mom was a quiet woman and took life as it came. She loved the Lord and I am sure that today she is resting in his ever-loving arms.

My Dad

When I was young, I remember my dad walking behind the horse and plow, from daybreak to the setting of the sun he labored in the field raising produce to sell. During the middle of the night, he drove to market to buy that which he could not raise and sell it in his roadside stand the following day.

Sometimes with great joy I went with him and lay my head on the seat to sleep, he would place his hat over my head to keep the glare of lights from disturbing my rest. I remember the smell of his hatband, objectionable to some I know, but to me that was my dad.

When to market we went during the heat of the day he would buy me a soda-pop from a washtub filled with ice, I can still taste that orange soda-pop and even today an orange soda-pop reminds me of the days of my youth.

In the fall of the year after the fields were put to rest dad would take a berth on one of the local fishing boats and plied the open sea in search of the catch of the day. When in port they came after a very long day at sea, they sold their catch for two to three cents a pound and if lucky, they got as much as a nickel a pound, not much by today's standards but back in the thirties and forties that was a enough to supply his family with their daily needs.

I remember the day that he let me go fishing with him and while at sea a storm arose while we were still far from shore. The wind blew a gale and the seas ran high and when the boat went down in a trough between two big seas I looked skyward and all I could see was a wall of water all around us (like looking up from the inside of a barrel and all one could see was the sky.). O how frightened I was, but dad assured me that everything would be alright and sure enough after many hours we entered the safety of the harbor where we were greeted by family and friends.

Sometimes during the warmth of the summer months we would live in a fishing shanty on the beach, many a good time we had working and playing by the edge of the sea. When the tide was low, dad would take us clamming and that night we would feast on steamed clams and fresh fish caught in the breaking surf. Dad taught us ways to live without having to have all of the comforts of home.

Dad worked hard long hours to raise a family of five children and never once do I recall him complaining or wanting to quit. He had a great love for our mom and he did his best to supply us all with our needs.

When World War II came along exempt was he. He took his carpentry tools in hand and worked for the government building army camps, first on Cape Cod and then in way off Virginia land. Dad was a man of many trades and did each one well, he never quibbled, he never complained, he did what he was called to do.

My dad was a man of small stature with a heart as big as the moon. In his later years he laid his labor aside and spent twenty

71

years in retirement with my mom by his side, their marriage was envied by many, for it was for life that they said, "I do."

Mom was the first to go and dad kind of died inside. He had lost the love of his life and sad was he. He lived on for another four years or so and when we laid him to rest I picked a red rose and laid it upon his silent chest, for you see he was my dad and I loved him so.

THANKS MOM

Thanks Mom for being there for me when I was young, before I was old enough to take care of myself you were there to guide me and correct me when I was wrong, you never let me down or let me overstep my bounds.

Times when I tried to bully my siblings or friends you corrected me and taught me to share my toys with those I didn't partially care for, you showed me that loving those I didn't like was more important than having my own way.

When I would come home with a bloody nose or skinned up knees you cleaned me up and gave me a big kiss and yet you let me know that fighting would get me nowhere but a spanking for being mean to those who I played with.

These were hard lessons to learn for one so young as I. Looking back on those times I now realize that you had my best interest at heart and just wanted me to learn that one has to share things in this life instead of being a know it all and always on the edge of being in trouble.

Mom, you were the one who saw to it on Sunday mornings that I went to Sunday School to learn about Jesus Christ and how an important role He plays in the lives of those who love and obey Him. It taught me to respect you and dad and be obedient to you both whether I wanted to or not, thanks, it really paid off when I entered the adult world, both at home and at work.

As I grew older and entered my teen years, you waited up at night until I came home and assured yourself that I was alright. If needed you showed me that even though I was old enough to be out at night I still needed to be held responsible for my actions, what you taught me back then still serve me well today.

In general Mom you guided me during my informative years, first, you showed me love, second, you disciplined me, third, you never let me down, forth, you stood by me and encouraged me to be the best I could be.

Mom, your love saw me through three long years in the service of my country. Your packages of cookies and goodies keep me in close contact with you and your concerns of safety for myself and my buddies. I still remember your tears as I boarded that train and went off to war and the tears of joy you shed when one night I awoke you from sleep and said, "Mom, I'm home."

When I found the woman who was to become my wife you opened your heart to her as if she was one of your own, you never tried to change her ways or interfere in our lives, you only encouraged us and gave us words of wisdom, I'm sure you had some things that you wanted to say that we might not like, but you kept them to yourself and in time things worked out.

When our first child was born you were the first to offer your help till my wife got back on her feet and able to take care of our first born by herself. You never criticized us for the mistakes we made in raising our children, you made us aware of them in other ways, ways that were gentle and loving.

Mom, it may sound as though I have made you out to be a perfect mother and grandmother, which we both know isn't the whole truth, for all mothers are fallible and more so are their children,. But, when one has had the loving relationship that we have had over the years goes a long way in overlooking the faults of the other and remembering the good times we have shared over the years.

Thanks Mom for being the loving mother that you have been, without your love and care I am sure my life would have been more trying than it has been, both me and my wife will always be in your debt for caring enough to share your unconditional love.

THE LEAF

Did you ever look at a leaf and see how God put it together? Each part of the leaf complements the other parts. From top to bottom of the leaf, there is one main artery up the middle of the leaf. There are smaller arteries that extend to each point of the leaf. There are smaller ones yet that go to other parts of the leaf. All of the arteries form the framework of the leaf; they are covered with a fiber-like substance that serves as collector cells for the function of the leaf.

The leaves act as evaporators for the benefit of the tree. Through the evaporation process, the leaves draw moisture from the ground through its root system. This in turn brings nutrients from the soil that nourishes the tree. Nutrients are the trees food source. The moisture-laden nutrients are drawn to all parts of the tree by the evaporation process of the leaves.

The leaves also take in carbon dioxide and give off oxygen. This process was put into operation by God to supply oxygen for not only man but for all of His creation. Everything on earth depends upon oxygen for its survival.

What a wonderful and intricate system God created when He created the leaf. If one part of this system is disturbed it affects the system as a whole. Man can produce oxygen through chemical means, but not enough to produce the needs of mankind. When the leaf is through its usefulness for the season, it drops to the ground and in time, it becomes a part of the food chain for the next season's growth of the tree. Nothing is lost in God's creation, it just takes different forms, depending on which stage it is in.

Without the leaf of all the trees and plants, man could not exist as he does now. God in His infinite wisdom created the leaf to produce oxygen for the benefit of mankind. Therefore, it behooves man to care for the trees and plants on this planet to ensure his own survival.

A Tribute To My Sunday Sschool Teacher

In my youth, my Sunday school teacher told me many stories about our Lord and Savior, Jesus Christ, stories that I still remember, stories that help me today when I begin to stray.

She told of how Jesus came to earth as a baby through a virgin birth, of how He loved all of the children of the world, of how He came so that you and I might one day live with Him for eternity.

Though I never fully understood I came to love Jesus because of the love she showed to me, I will always remember Miss Josephine Atkins as a kind, caring person, and one who loved the Lord and wanted the same for me.

Now that I am old and my hair has turned gray I still remember those days of my youth and the love Miss Atkins showed towards all of the children in her Sunday school class, not just me.

She encouraged us all to learn the scriptures and apply them to our lives, her smile still lightens my days, her voice I still hear as I open the Bible to read the word, she was indeed an angel sent by God to instill in all the need to have Jesus in our lives.

She loved all of her students the same and probably pondered in her heart if her words would have a lasting influence on our lives, well as for me I now know that she laid the foundation for the love I have for Jesus today.

Gentle and loving was she, over the years of my youth she planted the seeds that would one day grow and produce fruit fit for the Lord' table. Little did I know it then, but now that I am old I can look back and see her influence on my life and thank her for caring enough to care for me.

Though it was many years after her death that I turned my life over to Jesus I know in my heart that without her loving care I would not be the person that I am today, my struggles were long but somehow I know that she walked with me.

It takes a special person like Miss Josephine Atkins to bring the word of the Lord to a class of young people so that they one day would remember her fondly in their memories of the past.

Surly Miss Josephine Atkins was in heaven watching her young wards as they grew to maturity, praising God for the opportunity of planting the seeds of Christianity in the hearts of the youth in her Sunday school class.

MEMORIES

I can still smell the salt in the air as the
breezes blow from the sea to
the shore.

As a child I roamed the beaches and
played in the tide pools all
the day through.

Seagulls skimming across the ocean
waves, searching for their
next meal.

Sails of old passing in review, heading
for foreign lands, sailors in the
rigging reefing all sails
when the gales
blew.

Sounds of the roaring surf when the
nor'easters blew, shifting sand,
making new land where
no man has trod.

The mournful sound of the foghorn
warning ships to beware when
shrouded in fog.

The smell of flowers in the air as winter
gave way to the warmth of spring.

Return of the redwing blackbird singing
in its domain, signaling the return
of spring.

Picking the wildflowers for mother along
the path that leads towards home.

When the wind was right, the pungent
smell of the salt marsh was like
perfume to me.

Digging the succulent clams, catching
fish, hunting the deer, food
for all to share.

Revisiting places of my childhood, Grandparents who showered us with love
and tender care.

The excitement of the holidays when the
family gathered together from
far and near.

O to return to those days when we had
no cares, where are we going to
play tomorrow was the
biggest decision we
had to make.

To return home where we felt loved and
safe from our daily cares.

Unto you O lord we gather as we journey
back to our childhood days, still
trusting in You that our
tomorrows will be as
pleasant as our
yesterdays.

SEASONS COME AND GO

Outside of my window I watch as the seasons come and go. In the spring when the trees begin to leaf I hear the birds singing the songs of spring.

The flowers come forth all season through, their beauty displayed as the gentle rains wash their faces as skyward they gaze.

Farmers plow their fields and sow their seed, looking forward to a harvest of grain. The rest of us bask in the sunshine of summer, looking to the day when we can relax in old age.

As summer gives way to fall, God takes His paintbrush and with a dash of color turns the landscape into a painting of many colors. Its beauty displayed for all to see soon covers the ground with a carpet of many colors.

Then comes the day when the snows arrive, with laughter the children slide down the hills with squeals of delight, the cold air turning their fingers and toes cold and their noses red.

After the setting of the sun around the old fireplace, they gather to warm their fingers and toes. Sipping on warm cider and eating popcorn, they squeal with delight as they listen to Grandpa spinning tales of old. Then off to bed they go as Jack Frost paints pictures on the windowpanes.

This is also the season of the snowmobiles, they race across the open fields and into the woods, they go. Over the frozen lakes, they race and mountain tops too. Stopping only to warm themselves and eat by an open fire.

Then once again, the trees put on their leaves of green and the farmer plows his fields and plants his seed. Ever mindful man lives his life here on earth knowing that one day he too will have to leave his earthly home and return from whence he came, the arms of Jesus.

TEARS

———◦◦◦◦◦———

There are tears of joy that flow when we express
happiness, there are tears of sorrow
when we are sad.

We cry for joy, we cry for sorrow, but the tears are
the same.

They are but a liquid that is excreted from the eye
as we experience happiness or sorrow.

It is not the tear that makes us happy or sad, it is
the thought behind them that makes
them flow.

The tear stains the cheek as it flows, never more
to return, once released it has a journey
of its own.

A fulfillment of your will, a way of expressing
happiness or pain.

Its salty taste reminds us of the ocean as all salt
taste the same.

The Indian who sat beside the sea and mourned
the loss of his land shed tears of sorrow.

The sailor's wife who lost her love at sea relieved
her sorrow by crying an endless
stream of tears.

The little boy or girl who stubbed their toe was
consoled by their mother after shedding
tears of pain.

The bride who cried for joy as she said, "I do.", or
the mother who shed tears of joy when her
child was born.

All who stood at Calvary shed tears as the life drained
from our Lord, Jesus.

Put all of these together and what do you have, the
tears of time that never change.

Tears are one of God' wonders that allow us to release
our feelings and begin to heal.

Healing begins when we release that first salty drop
showing either happiness or pain.

Though the tears can be many or few, it is not the
amount that matters so much as it is the fact
that we can release them and relieve
the strain.

God surly knew what he was doing when He gave us
the endless supply of tears that we are able
to release on command.

As they run down your cheek, taste them and remember
who gave them to you.

The tear is but an expression of self, it combines all of
our feelings into one little drop of fluid we
call a tear.

It relieves us of our heartaches and pain, with it goes
our hurts and we are able to smile again.

Hold not back your tears; be proud that you have them
to give, release them and in return, they will
release you of the strain of you burdens.

Fear them not, they are meant to help you, not harm,
happy is the person who can release them.

A God given gift for you and me, a gift too precious to
hold inside, they are always there when you
need them, just a few or a lot.

Again, thank God for your tears and know that He too
has them in abundance when we go astray.

THAT TIME OF YEAR AGAIN

I t was that time of year again, time to take the scallop dredges from storage and make the necessary repairs before the upcoming season. They had hung in their usual place in the chicken coop. This year would be somewhat special because my three children were now old enough so that on good days they would be able to go with me. Of course, they would only go one at a time.

It seemed like only yesterday that my father had taken me scalloping for the first time. What a thrill that was, it made me feel all grown up. With boots that were three times too big and the rain gear that was too big, but they would serve their purpose well. They kept me dry while I helped dad cull the scallops from the rest of the debris that was brought up by the dredges. I even had to stand on an upside down bucket in order to be high enough to reach the culling board.

At times, the dredges caught some fish as they were dragged across the scallop beds. Like any other child I did not want to throw the fish back into the water, so I talked my dad into letting me keep the fish in a bucket of water. I would play with the fish by the hour and even try to feed them some of my lunch, wondering why they never ate any of it. Being too young to realize that fish did not necessarily like our kind of food and besides that, they were out of their natural environment.

When the limit of scallops were caught and it was time to head for home father always made me dump my pet fish overboard so that they could live and grow to be mature fish. I could not understand why I could not take them home with me, I even promised to take care of them, but to no avail. The only ones we kept were those that were big enough to have as a family meal, this used to bring tears to my eyes to think that I had to eat the fish that I had been playing with. It just did not seem fair somehow.

Then dad would try to explain about how things were and that fish were for us to eat and enjoy as a food and not as pets. Needless to say, his explanation did not make much sense to me, but in a sense, I felt real grown up because we had caught some fish that we could take home and have for a meal.

There were also many crabs that were caught in the dredges and they were a lot of fun to play with too. Poking them with an empty shell or something else and they in turn biting back and even at times putting my finger too close to the crab's claws and having the crab bite my finger or the gloves that I had on.

When I got older and was in high school my father let me take his boat after school and go scalloping with it by myself. He had gone early in the day and got his limit and would be at home opening his catch of the day while I was catching my limit. At that time, a limit consisted of five bushels. When the tide was low in the afternoon after school, I would go down to the river and wade around with my skiff in tow and pick up scallops and get as many as possible before the tide was too high to wade anymore. This was one way that I made my spending money. It was as much fun to get the scallops this way, as it was to use the big boat and the dredges.

One time I used the big boat, after catching my limit of scallops I went to shore and unloaded my catch, and then I put the boat back on its mooring. When I went to get into the skiff to row ashore the skiff started to drift away from the boat, I had one foot in the big boat and one foot in the skiff and as the two drifted apart, I found myself straddling between the two and after losing my balance, I ended up in the water. Grabbing a hold of the skiff, I started to make my way to shore when I heard someone laughing. Looking around I saw my uncle standing on the shore doubled up in laughter. It was funny to him, but to me it was embarrassing. After reaching close enough to shore to where I could touch bottom I waded the rest of the way to shore. Then I too began to laugh about the whole incident. I was in no danger, it was because of the fact that I had allowed the two boats to drift apart and I ending up in the water.

I had many good times down at the shore when I was growing up and now they are precious memories. Memories when I had nothing to do but have fun and play. To go shell fishing when I had need of some money or when mom wanted shellfish for a meal. Through growing up and around the water, I have a great love for the sea and a great respect for the sea. I cherish the times when I took my children scalloping as my father had taken me. To once again live by and enjoy the sea would be all right with me.

KILDEE HILL

Atop of Kildee Hill stands a water tower, in
its shadow is the house where my
my Grandfather was born.

The house where his father before him lived
and died, the barn where his father
stabled his horse and buggy
when he was not away
ministering to the
sick and dying
still stands.

Great-grandfather Phillips picked his herbs
and mixed them well, along with a
prayer he ministered to all
in need.

So successful was he that all around
called him "Doctor" wherever
he was called.

From Great-grandfather to Grandfather
the property did pass, my father
was born in the same
bedroom that his
father before
him was
born.

Looking to the south one can see
Allen's harbor and the south
bay beyond.

The old Doane House across the road
with its Widow Walk bears
witness to the days of
sail of long ago.

Visions of a sea Captain's wife pacing
the Widows Walk searching the
horizon for a glimpse of
his ship sailing up
the bay.

All road traffic passes over Kildee Hill,
at night the auto lights shine
in the windows as
they pass by.

During the winter months Grandpa built
his windmills and had them ready
for display when the weather
did warm.

Bright and gay they did stand as sentinels
of the past, for the tourist to purchase
when they passed by.

Sisson Road could be seen to the west, on
its corner stood Howard Johnson'
restaurant and ice cream store.

As kids we hurried down the hill to partake
of the twenty-eight flavors, it boasted of.

To the north, at the foot of the hill were the
apple trees that bore the fruit that
gave us bellyaches when too
many we did eat.

Back to Grandma we did run and willingly
partook of some awful tasting remedy
to relieve the pain.

We also found Oak leaves that we chewed to
do as Grandpa did, and spit its juice
as far as we could.

Kildee Hill like all other places change with
time, but the memories we made as
children come to mind whenever
I recall the days I spent at
Grandpa and Grandma'
house atop of
Kildee Hill.

Memories Of Yesteryears

-----∞∞∞-----

Standing on a high bluff overlooking the expanse of the ocean with a gentle breeze blowing in my face, the fragrance of the salt air stirred memories of my days spent at sea. It sets aflame glowing embers of yesteryears. Times of joy and times of sorrow when my shipmates and I fought the furry of Nature trying to survive great storms at sea. Memories of shipmates, who were not as fortunate as I, now sleep in the briny deep. O what tales they could spin if only their voices could be heard.

On stormy nights, I can still hear my shipmates crying out against the gales that turned the sea into a foaming mass of hell. Tossing their ship to and fro, trying to bury them with green angry mountainous seas. The groaning of ships timbers and the cracking of a mast unable to stand the strain of sails filled with the blusterous winds. Many a ship succumbed to the fury of the sea and carried their crew to their watery grave.

Then there were times when the sea was a seaman's best friend, it provided them with a life of adventure. A place to be free, unencumbered by the limitations of life on land. Free to roam the world and taste the delicacies that were to be found in ports of foreign lands. The sea could feed you as well as feed upon you, a mistress to both love and to hate, depending upon her mood.

94

The cry of a gull as it passed overhead brought me back to reality. My days at sea had ended for I was now too old to climb the rigging of those great ladies of the sea. Never more would I enter a foreign port and partake of the festivities that a sailor enjoys. Approaching storms now cause my weary bones great discomfort where once they brought a challenge to survive. My eyes have grown dim and can no longer drink in the beauty and the horrors of the sea. The sea, a place where I had spent the most of my life and knew its every mood.

My wife left this earth several years ago while I was at sea, now my life is hollow with only memories of her beauty and the love she showed towards me. Now this old world holds only fond memories for men like me. We wander the shore exchanging yarns of times gone by; shake hands with old shipmates as one by one they slip away. We had our yesterdays when we sailed the world around, our tomorrows look bleak, with only memories of the deep. As we watch the sunsets, we wonder if we will see tomorrow's sunrises. We are at the point of life that we realize that just as life began it must also end.

So, we turn and walk towards our future just as we had done when we were young. We sail in hope and faith towards the one who put us here and know that that journey will have peaceful skies and calm seas, untouched by the horrors that we once knew. The next sunrise that we will see will be over a land and sea that we now cannot see. Peaceful and quiet it will be, without any more storms at sea.

Remember

—⦿—

O Lord as the days of my life come to an end I remember my youth when all things were fun, I remember running over the fields and playing that I was an Indian boy living by the edge of the sea.

Times when I dug the succulent clams that my mother made into a clam pie or a clam chowder, how tasty they were as the family gathered around the table and gave thanks to God for another meal.

Times seemed hard at the time but looking back, they were good times, in the spring of the year father worked in the fields planting the crops that he would sell in his roadside stand, us boys worked in the fields too, not always to our liking, but a chore that had to be done.

The girls helped mother in the house and many afternoons during the summer, we were allowed to go swimming in a nearby lake. Often time's mother would have to come and get us, with our skin wrinkled from being in the water all afternoon we walked home with a towel around us to warm us.

Some summers we lived in a fishing shanty on the beach and came off the beach during the daytime to work the fields with father and then return to our summer home late in the afternoon. While on the beach, we played with the shore birds and watched as their young hatched from their eggs or played by the ocean's edge. Something that today is against the law to go on the beach without special permission from some government department.

Our pay for helping father work the fields was to pick out some new clothes from the Sears and Roebuck catalog to wear to school in the fall, now that was a big deal to have new clothes to wear to school.

After graduating from school, we had no choice but to join a branch of service for World War 11 was raging the world around. I joined the Army Air Corp and served as an aircraft mechanic. A real change for many a country boy who had never been away from home before, but endure we did and after victory, I returned home.

Three years later, I married and had three children when things turned for the worse and our marriage ended in divorce. Then came the turbulent years when another marriage fell apart and my lust for sin almost consumed me. I am not proud of those turbulent years for I did much that I would have not done if I had had a stable marriage. For several years, I was lost in the sea of sin and loved every minute of it until it brought me to the brink of destroying myself by the way that I was living life.

After giving up on ever having a loving and stable marriage God arraigned a meeting with my present wife. We have been married now for thirty-three years. During this time, God has allowed me to see the "Light" of His Son, Jesus Christ, and this changed my life forever and my outlook on life. I know for a fact that if it had not been for the love that God has for me I would not have survived my turbulent years. Much transpired during those turbulent years, much I have written about in some of my other writings.

Though I am now in my eighties, I still work forty hours a week, am in good health, and will probably continue to work until this old body gives out. Not a bad way to be, just wish that I could have a little more leisure time. Memories are precious, even the bad ones have served me well when it comes to solving some of lives' problems.

I have been a witness to many things in my life and know that the best things in life come from God and are intended to better our lives and bring us closer to Him. The best advice that I can pass on to anyone is to cultivate a good relationship with God and accept His Son, Jesus Christ, as his or her Lord and Savior. This will not deter the trials of life but it will give one a place of refuge when the storms of life rage. It will also give one a place to seek the answers to daily problems and make life easier.

THE MOUNTAINS

Head for the mountains boys where the streams are pure
and clean, the moose, deer and bear roam free.

Head for the mountains boys where the stars are bright and
you can hear the call of the owl and the whippoorwill.

Head for the mountains boys where the chipmunk scurries
for cover when the eagle soars overhead, the trees
stand tall and the streams run free.

Head for the mountains boys where the beaver builds his
dam and trout abound.

Head for the mountains boys where the mountaintops meet
the sky, regret not your decision to leave all behind
to seek peace of mind.

Head for the mountains boys where in the winter everything
is covered with a blanket of snow, then cabin bound
we will be.

Head for the mountains boys where spring brings new life
to the land, the fawn and bear cubs frolic and play,
and all of God's creatures renew their kind.

Head for the mountains boys where the lighting flashes and
the thunder echoes from peak to peak, far below you
can observe mankind struggling to be free.

Head for the mountains boys when you feel the need to be
alone and commune with our maker who created all,
leave all of your cares behind and there live free.

Head for the mountains boys and prepare yourselves for
that new life to come, before it is time to leave all
behind and join your mountain friends, who
now observe the mountain peaks
from on high.

THE OLD SENTINAL

After rounding the point of Monomoy I look
to the northeast to see if I can see
your beacon of light winking
at me.

Your light gave me a ray of hope after being
battered by an angry sea.

As I appraoched the shelter of Hardings Beach
where the sea no longer raged I felt the
warmth you had for me.

You have guided many a seaman over the years
to the safety of Stage Harbor when the seas
were running high.

The only time your light did not shine was
during the war years when all fought
to remain free.

Even then on moon-lite nights your profile
could be seen from far down the bay.

Many a fisherman has prayed to see your
light while they were still navagating
the storm tossed bay.

\You were and still are a sentinal of hope of
those who ply the waters of the bay
when the winds are contrary.

Once sighted many a seaman has adjusted
his course and soon found themselves
in the shelter of your lee.

Then came the day when the powers to be
decided to put you to rest.

They snuffed your light and replaced it with
one that no one had to clean.

After the change over they abanconed you
and left you to decay.

Your light was removed and placed in a
museum for all to see.

Never more wuld your light be seen and
never more would you guide
bedragled seamen home.

Your replacement might well do the job,
but never will it be the same.

The passage of an era had arrived, but
the young will never undestaznd
how much you meant to the
seaman caught in a gale
while braving the
storms of
the bay.

After years of abandenment one came along
and restored the Light Keepers home
and painted your tower white.

All may be back as it was, but your light
no longer shines in fair weather as
well as foul.

Even without your light you are still a
sentinal of hope to the seamen
coming up the bay.

Now, all who walk Hardings Beach or
swim in the waters of the bay, look
up and admire you for what
you used to be.

Although your light will never shine
again, you are still a semtinal of
hope to those who brave
the waters of the bay.

THE WIND

Let the wind blow O Lord, let it blow wherever it will.
Where does it come from and where does it go?
Only God knows the answers to
the unknown.

It can blow gentle, warm the earth in the spring, so
that she might bring forth her beauty sublime.

The ships at sea run before the breezes, it warms the
hearts of the sailors when they climb the rigging
and release the sails that billow and drives
them ever onward.

The birds soar far and wide on the currents of air that
blow from place to place, never stopping,
always on the move.

The fragile seeds of the wildflowers are scattered hither
and yon by the breath of the wind.

Taking root wherever they land as the seasons come and
go, spreading beauty wherever they grow.

To the delight of the children, the wind keeps their kites
tugging at their strings, dancing high overhead.

The farmer tosses his grains before the wind and the
chaff is blown away.

The windmills mighty arms turn with delight, grinding the
grains that waved in the winds of yesterday.

The wind creates a draft in the chimney and carries the smoke
of the fire high into the air, leaving the heat
of the flame behind.

Always doing its assigned task, never looking for a place to
rest, pushing the clouds hither and yon, driving
the rains that water the meadows and fields.

Sometimes violently driving the foam covered waves,
dashing ships upon the rocky shores.

When angry the winds can cause havoc with all that is in its
way, roar like a lion and be just as brave.

Even though it cannot be seem, it sure can be heard and let
you know who is in charge, obedient only to one,
the hand of God.

It can create pleasure by driving the sailboat with its mighty
hand and it can destroy when on a rampage it goes.

To please the wind we cannot, but live with the wind we must,
whether it be for good or whether it be for bad
we know not until it has passed.

To be without it would be a catastrophe for all, in the spring it
dries the land, in the summer it helps to keep us cool,
in the fall it scatters the leaves, in the
winter it blows cold and drives
the snows.

Even though the winds cannot be seen and they blow wherever
they please, without them we would be hard pressed
to keep this old world clean.

WHERE DID THE CAT GO

The new barn was finished; all of my plumbing supplies had been transferred from the old barn and put in their proper place. The new barn had room for four vehicles, all of my plumbing supplies, a big woodworking shop, plus ten cord of firewood, which I used to heat the woodworking shop and the main house. It also had a second floor, which could be used for storage or whatever else I might, have a need of. The building was forty feet by sixty feet with a second floor.

The foundation of the barn was installed just after the frost was out of the ground in the early spring and the roof was finished two days before the first snow of the winter. Weekend carpenters that consisted of neighbors, friends from Massachusetts, and Connecticut came together for a barn raising and built the barn. A good friend from Massachusetts was in the construction business and he served as the supervisor on the job. Some weekends there where as many as thirty willing hands to cut materials, carry materials, pound nails, and whatever else that needed to be done. The women prepared the food and served it. There was no beer or alcohol allowed until after working hours, then every man for themselves. I supplied all of the food and beer, plus a place to sleep for those who did not have a place. Some weekend's people were stacked like cordwood, all over the house, sleeping on the floor mostly. There were no injuries on the job from the time I started to build the barn until its completion.

It took a total of twenty one thousand feet of lumber to construct the barn, all of it was purchased from a local sawmill at nineteen cents a square foot, amounting to a cost of three thousand nine hundred and ninety dollars. It was all of White Pine and ranged from two by fours to two by fourteen timbers that were used for stair stringers. It was all cut to oversize and had very few knots in them, too good to build a barn with, more suited for making furniture or for craftwork than a barn. The foundation of the barn was made of treated pressure wood, made into panels four feet by eight feet and was the first wooden foundation in the area. The panels were set three and a half feet in the ground. The whole worksite looked more like a lumberyard with the different size lumber stacked everywhere.

The old barn was attached to the house with a door in the kitchen that allowed access to the barn without going outside during the winter months. There was two other sheds off the barn plus a chicken house off the last shed. All were assessable during the winter without going outside. These out sheds and chicken house were torn down to make room for the new barn. The old barn also had a second floor for the storage of hay and a basement of sorts with a dirt floor and a large door to the outside. Being below ground there was a dug down area in front of the big door, enough to allow a horse drawn wagon to go in and out. In one corner of the barn on the first floor was a three hole outhouse for family use before they had inside plumbing. Both the cow manure and human waste was stored in the cellar of the barn until spring when the old timers loaded it on a wagon and spread it on the hay fields as fertilizer. In those days, the farmers wasted nothing and everything had a use.

In the kitchen of the farmhouse was a water-box made of stone and motor with a wooden top to keep things from falling into the household water supply. It held from forty to sixty gallons of water and was gravity fed from a dug well in the woods behind the house. From the water-box, an overflow pipe lead to the outside of the kitchen, thus a fresh supply of water was available in the kitchen all of the time. In the dug-well, the old timers would put a trout to eat all and any bugs that might get into the well. The water from that well was always cold and refreshing. This water supply was in use when I bought the property in nineteen sixty-five and was used until I put in an artesian well.

When I found out that the property was for sale, I approached the old couple that owned it about buying it. The husband told me that his parents had owned the place and had raised their family there. At first, they had only a one-room cabin and when their family out grew the cabin, they bought an old house that was several miles away, moved it, and added it to the cabin in nineteen hundred and one. The main house had a total of nine rooms, five rooms on the first floor and four bedrooms on the second floor. The one-room cabin became the kitchen; it was open to the roof with a sleeping loft at one end. The outside of the house had a stucco finish, it became known as the "Stucco Cottage", and there was a sign on the front of the house with the name on it. Both the house and cabin dates back to the late eighteen hundreds.

There were seven acres of land that went with the house and his asking price was seven thousand dollars. During our conversation, I asked if there was any other land that he would consider selling with the house. After hesitating for a few minutes he told me that he had an additional seventy eight acres that abutted the seven acres, quickly he added that he had recently timbered that piece of land and that really it was not that much good for anything. He added that all it had left was young growth trees and it was rocky and high ground. It formed one side of a valley that ran through that area. After a while, I asked if he would let it go with the original seven acres and the house and how much he wanted for the additional seventy-eight acres. Again, he hesitated for a while and finally said that he guessed that he would have to have an additional fifteen hundred dollars seeing as how it was not prime land. My first thoughts to myself were, "Man, you just sold yourself a piece of land." I was all excited inside, but tried not to show it on the outside.

Naturally, I agreed to the price and agreed to buy the extra land. This made a total of eight five hundred dollars for eight five acres of land with the farmhouse. He did not want to sell me a "Pig in the poke" as he put it so we arranged that he would walk the boundaries with me the following day. I met Harold Fogg the next day at our appointed time and together we walked the boundaries. Needless to say, I had no idea where we were except for being in the woods following Harold around. The boundaries were marked with stonewalls except for the East boundary and that was marked with a wire fence. The fence had been there for years as the trees had grown around the wire and now ran through the middle of the trees. The old timers never cut the boundary trees so as not to lose the location of the boundaries. There was quite a variety of trees, including white pine, oak, beech, white birch, gray birch and hemlock. He showed me a location where there was once a logging camp around the turn of the century. There was nothing left of the camp itself, except for a piece of the cook stove and a part of the waterline that supplied water to the camp. In another location, Harold showed me where someone had blasted into the ledge in search of mica. They had found some but not enough to continue mining it. We came across another location where there was an outcrop of ledge that overlooked the valley. It was a beautiful spot and a few years later, I built a camp on that site. Many years later the camp was struck by lighting and burned to the ground. As far as I was concerned, Harold did not have to give me a guided tour of the property for I had already made up my mind to buy it.

After coming out of the woods we went to the farmhouse, which was in somewhat of a rundown condition as it had not, been lived in for quite some time. There was a kitchen, dining room, living room with a fireplace, bedroom, bath and small office on the first floor and four bedrooms on the second floor. Harold wanted to show me the basement, but when he opened the door to the basement, we saw that it had about four feet of water in it. The building was structurally sound so these minor details did not bother me that much, besides that where could I find eighty-five acres of land with a house on it for that kind of money.

Over the next few years, I remolded the house and in so doing, I had to tear down some of the walls and ceilings. When the walls and ceilings were opened, it became quite apparent where the strange smell was coming from, especially when the humidity was high. For the most part they were packed with rat and mice pellets along with skeletons of mice, rats, squirrels and corncobs. I even found a secret hiding place in one of the walls. I am sure that this was where the old folks kept their valuables and money instead of using a bank as we do today. Just about the only time they went to town was to buy staples such as flower, sugar, coffee and such. They raised most of everything else, beef, chickens, pigs and etc. The old kitchen was large enough so that when I remolded it I use one end of it as a master bath for the downstairs bedroom and still had plenty of room to make a more modern kitchen. One of the bedrooms on the second floor was made into a bathroom for the second floor.

During this time, I had a farm pond built just west of the house, what was once low ground was built up to form the pond. It made a good swimming hole during the summer months and a good place to skate during the winter, until the snow got too deep to skate. I put a few goldfish in the pond, in no time; they grew to be ten to twelve inches long and in a couple of years there was what seemed like hundreds of them.

During the winter months we spent our leisure time snowmobiling. We spent many a day snowmobiling as we could go anywhere we wanted over the different snowmobile trails, as far as twenty miles or more without going onto the roads. We did a lot of snowmobiling at night and more than one night we never got home until the small hours of the morning. Weekends we took our food with us and would stop on a lake or in the woods and build a fire to cook our hot-dogs and such on. Sometimes we would have as many as twenty to thirty machines, all trailing one another. If we got back to the house early, we started a fire in the fireplace and just sat enjoying the fire with popcorn and such. Even so, as spring approached we were glad to see the winter end.

When the price of heating oil got too expensive to buy, we heated the old farmhouse with wood. In the spring or early summer we went into the woods, cut enough trees down, and left them there to season, in the fall we hauled the trees out the woods and cut and split them, then stacked them in the barn for use during the winter. In all we burned ten cords of wood per winter, which meant that it took a lot of time and energy to get ready for winter. As it is said, "Wood will warm you six times. When you cut the tree down, when you hauled the wood out of the woods, when you cut it up and split it, when you stacked it in the barn, when you carried it into the house and when you cleaned out the ashes and took them outside." Fortunately, when friends came for the weekend they helped to do much of the hard work of burning wood.

During one winter I recall the snow in the open fields got be close to ten feet in depth, where the plows plowed the snow on the roads the snow was plowed so high that one could not see an automobile going down the road. The farmhouse had a metal roof, which allowed the snow to slide off the roof and there was times when I had to shovel the snow away from the windows to allow the sunlight to come into the house. On other occasions, the snow built up against the house so high that one could walk up the snow bank and step down onto the roof. When the outside temperature was down around zero and there was no wing blowing, I have gone outside with just a tee shirt and shoveled snow to clear the walkway to the house and barn. I lived in New Hampshire for fifteen years and only once or twice do I recall the wind blowing during a snowstorm. During a snowstorm, the snow just floated down and resembled a winter wonderland, but after the storms were over the wind would blow for a couple of days and this is what would make the snowdrifts high. Snow also served as insulation as it piled up against the houses. I have gone to work in the morning with the temperature at forty degrees below zero and worked out in it all day. It wasn't very pleasant but when I had work, I never missed a day's work because of the snow conditions or temperature. Sometimes I used these excesses to take a day off to go snowmobiling or ice fishing.

Some days while snowmobiling, we would go to Laconia for lunch, which was eighteen miles from where we lived. Local snowmobile clubs kept the trails groomed. Many of the trails went across the frozen lakes and while on the lakes one go as fast as they wanted. The fastest I have been on a snowmobile was eighty-five miles an hour and have turned one over doing fifty miles an hour while in a tight turn without getting hurt. During any given year several people do get hurt and even some are killed while riding beyond their abilities or from going too fast, while on trails through the woods or going on the lakes before the ice is sufficient to keep from giving way. Snowmobiling is as safe or dangerous as you want to make it.

One story I can tell occurred at night while crossing a lake on a snowmobile. Eight of us had gone to a local restaurant by snowmobile for dinner. After dinner, we decided to go for a ride on our snowmobiles before heading for home. My wife and I were the last in line, each on our own machine went out on the lake across from the restaurant. We all stayed on the same trail as was customary when traveling in a group. Unknown to us there was a soft spot in the ice and as the machines in front of us crossed this area, it became too weak to support us when it was our turn to cross that weak spot. The ice gave way and my wife who was in front of me broke though the ice and started to sink into the water. As soon as I saw her do this I turned off the trail, went around her, and stop on solid ice just in front of her. As I stepped off my machine, I too broke through the ice. Thoughts of being in the water and not being able to get out flashed through my mind. Thankfully, there was solid ice about twelve inches below the surface of the top ice and it was strong enough to support us. It often happens that there are two layers of ice with water in between. Neither one of us panicked, but it was quite apparent that my wife was about to. I walked a few feet with water almost up to my knees and helped my wife to solid ice, and then I went back, started her machine, and worked it back to solid ice and safety. In the meanwhile, the rest of our group had stopped about a half-mile distant and was waiting for us to catch up with them, unaware that she had gone through the ice. They were about to come back in search of us when we caught up with them. It was quite an experience, especially for my wife as she is from Mississippi and knew nothing about the hazards of snowmobiling. After that when we went out with a group we kept closer contact with one another.

My son and I had a similar experience a few years before that when one time while on the same lake, but a different area. We did not go through the ice so much as the top ice was thin and it just bellied down and water came up around us, but we were able to keep going and get back onto solid ice. None of our group ever got into serious trouble, but we all had our scares.

Another time while coming back from Laconia, we crossed one of the lakes and my son and a friend of his went off the lake in the wrong place and found themselves on top of a big boulder with a drop of ten feet on the other side. They were able to stop in time, turned around, went back to the lake, and found the right place to exit the lake. The rest of us came along a few minutes later ad my wife took their trail off the lake thinking that it was the right trail. The only problem was that she never stopped when she reached the top of the boulder. She went off the top of the boulder and found herself in mid air with no place to go but down. There was tree in her way and when she hit it she went one way and her machine the other way, this is probably why she never got seriously hurt. The depth of the snow cushioned her fall and she was able to get up and finish the trip home. Neither she nor her machine was any the worse for that flying trip, except the machine had a bent ski. The next day she had a big shiner and a banged up knee along with a sore back that lasted for a few days.

Another event that became a yearly tradition at the old farmhouse was New Years Eve. It started out like any other New Year's party and in a couple years, it became a tradition. Some of our friends would come a week before the party and together we would set up a bonfire. We cut and stacked wood to at least ten feet in height, and then on New Year's Eve we would torch it off. We started the fire about two hours before midnight and by the time; the New Year tolled in the flames would reach twenty to thirty feet into the air, lighting the whole valley up. From a distance, it looked as though the house was on fire.

The last year that we had the bonfire, things rather got out of hand. There were at least seventy-five people show up for the yearly event and a lot of them we did not even know. Therefore, we decide not to have such a big party again, mainly so that no one would get hurt or fall into the fire from having too much hooch. This was a wise decision on our part.

Another winter sport was racing cars on the frozen lakes, they would plow a quarter mile oval track and as many as twenty cars at a time would race. The onlookers would drive their cars on the ice and park all around the track to watch them race. The race cars had chains on their wheels and before the races were over there would be holes in the ice in the corners and water would flood the corners of the track.

Somehow, I got away from what I first started to write about, "WHERE DID THE CAT GO". The biggest problem left after moving all of my plumbing supplies into the new barn was, there were way too many cats living in the old barn that I did not want to have in the new barn. As many as twenty cats had made the old barn their home. They raised their offspring there and they did not intend to move out even though the barn was in the process of being torn down.

We managed to give away some of them, but a lot of them were so wild that there was no way of catching them, so much to my chagrin on weekends when my friend Ed Proudfoot came up from the Cape he helped me to shoot them till finally we got down to one cat. Well, that cat had no intentions of being shot and somehow avoided that kind of fate. Finally, the cat moved into the new barn and made itself right at home. It still managed to avoid the inevitable, as it seemed to sense when it was being hunted and kept from sight. One weekend when Ed was there, we saw it go into the new barn and up to the second floor. Well, it was now or never, while I went to the house for the gun Ed kept an eye on the barn doors to make sure the cat did not leave. When I returned with the gun, we decided to open the window on the landing of the stairs that went to the second floor. Ed stood outside where he could see the open window while I went up stairs to chase the cat down the stairs and when the cat went out the window Ed would shoot it. I went into the barn and closed all of the doors so that the only place the cat could go was out of the open window. After reaching the second floor, I could not find the cat so I began to hit the floor with a stick and soon the cat came out of its hiding place and began to run around. It did not take too long before the cat ran down the stairs and out the open window the cat went. About then I heard the gun go off and I said to myself, "Well I guess that's the end of that cat."

About then I heard Ed begin to laugh and for the life of me, I could not imagine what he was laughing about. I hurried down the stairs and outside where Ed was, about this time Ed was doubled over in laughter. After a few minutes, Ed calmed down and explained what had happened. After I had called, down to Ed that the cat was headed down the stairs, he pointed the gun towards the window and when the cat came out through the window, he fired the gun. He had missed the cat and shot the electric light meter that was next to the window. The cat ran off into the woods and was never seen again and is probably still running. The next couple of months the electric bill for the barn was nothing until the light company replaced the meter Ed had shot. It did not break the meter enough so that the electricity was disconnected; it just failed to record any usage. We never did know where the cat ended up, but we sure had many a laugh about the dead electric meter. So ends the story of "WHERE DID THE CAT GO."

SIGNS OF FALL

I walked the woodland paths in silence and serenity with
the beauty and wonders of nature all around.

I stopped and listened to the sounds of the rustling
leaves as the gentle breezes blew.

I heard the acorns as they hit the ground like a falling
rain, I witnessed the chipmunks scurrying, hiding
their stores for the winter to come.

The summer birds were gone and the cry of the
blue jay was all that one could hear.

An occasional woodpecker could be heard in the distance
searching out a meal from beneath the bark of a tree.

The woodland ferns had turned brown and would
soon become a part of the earth beneath.

The autumn leaves floating on the pond formed a
colorful patchwork quilt fit for a queen.

The tasty partridge berries hung in clumps of two or
three, just waiting to be picked and savored
by you and me.

In the distance the deer stands under the apple
tree feeding on its fruit.

The autumn leaves in all their splendor sparkle
in the noonday sun.

Their beauty is unsurpassed as the last rays of the
setting sun exposes their beauty for all to see.

The fox and the raccoon leave their tracks in the
soft sands of their domain.

Even the skunks have their place in the scheme of
things, although sometimes we disagree.

In the far distance the cry of the shore birds could
be heard as they soared over the breaking seas.

God's hand has surly been at work this day,
painting the leaves and in general keeping
things the way they had ought to be.

The Lilac Bush

Behind grandma's house stands a stately lilac bush.

It is nourished by the waters of heaven and the tender
love of one who cares.

When the cold chill of winter has passed and the warm
days of spring have arrived it sends forth the buds
of flowers yet to arrive.

Everyone waits in anticipation of their fragrant smell.

When picked and carried inside, their fragrance fills the
whole house and drives the musty odors of
winter away.

They make an appropriate spring bouquet to set before
the headstones of loved ones who have
passed away.

The beauty of the Lilac and its fragrance is enjoyed by
all and lifts hearts to a new high.

When the lilac bush blooms, it ushers in a new season,
one full of hope for that which is to come.

Whether they be of the white variety or of the purple
makes no never mind, because the lilac bush
is a gift from God to man.

The Sea

The sea is as endless as time and its depths
are as deep as the highest mountains.

Its waters are restless and always on the
move, when the storms rage the
wind whips its waters into
a foaming mass.

The raging seas can devastate everything
in its path, neither man nor ship
can survive its fury if it
chooses to do
them in.

As the angry sea beaks upon the shore
it can move mountains of sand
from place to place.

Man has tried to tame the angry seas
and has yet to prevail, for the
power of the angry sea
cannot be tamed by
the hand of man.

When at times the winds cease to blow
the sea is as a looking glass, only
the tide ripples the surface
of the deep.

When at night the moon-beams dance
across the surface of the deep
they dazzle lovers walking
along the shore.

From its depths, man harvests its bounties
and supplies his family with
their needs.

He sails the seven seas in search of treasure
beyond his dreams.

Many a soul has died on such ventures, never
to see their loved ones ever more.

Their bodies committed to the deep until the
day of resurrection, then their souls
shall rise and forever be free
from their watery grave.

On moonlit nights ghost ships have been
seen sailing without sails upon
a glassy sea.

Their seamen singing songs of old melodic
tunes, heard only by the ears of
the dead.

In its fury and in its glory the sea will always
be a place of fascination for those who
live and love the adventure of
living by the sea.

TO THOSE WHO CONTEMPLATE DIVORCE

Divorce is not the answer, especially where children are involved. The children are the ones who get hurt the most because of a divorce. Their world is shattered from the loss of the presence of both parents in the same home. The children are asked and sometimes forced to take sides with one parent or the other. Children, especially young children are not mature enough to understand what is going on, let alone taking sides. Children have enough problems growing up without being forced to take on the problems of their parents' divorce. These are the years that all the children should have on their minds is who are they going to play with, going to see their grandparents, waiting for mommy or daddy coming home from work. These are the years that the young children bond with their parents and form relationships with them that will last a lifetime.

Where there was at one time enough love between two people to marry, then that love should be strong enough to weather the hard times that occur during a marriage. Marriage is a scarred institution given of God and should be entered into with this in mind.

Parenthood is a lifelong endeavor and the welfare of the children should be at the top of the list of one's priorities. Once a child is grown and or married then the parents role changes to one of support without interfering in their child's life unless asked by the child to do so. This does not mean that one should abandon their child and not help them when they are in need, but it does mean that the parent does not have the right to meddle in their children's lives. There is a difference between helping and meddling.

Many marriages are doomed to failure even before the marriage, just because the reason for the marriage is not right in the first place. Some of these wrong reasons are; to get out of an unhappy home life, pregnancy, lust for money, lust for social status, are but a few. Every time the Biblical values of marriage are left out of the marriage then that marriage is in trouble even before it begins. The pains of divorce can and sometime does last a lifetime.

There is no acceptable reason for divorce except for the one given in the Bible, it can be found in Matthew 5:32. Even then, the marriage can work if the offended party is willing to forgive and the offending party wants the marriage to survive. If neither party does not want the marriage to survive then that marriage is doomed. It takes both parties to make a marriage work.

All parties involved in a divorce, including both sets of parents of the divorcing couple and all other family members are affected by that divorce. Divorce can and does split families and friends right down the middle and creates hardships for all involved. In the long run no one wins in a divorce, everyone is a looser, especially the children. To remarry where there are existing children adds stress to that marriage right from the beginning and often times that marriage will fail also.

Marriage is a lifetime commitment and should not be entered into for the wrong reasons. It is better not to marry at all, than it is to marry and have children and end up in divorce. The breakup of the family unit is one the basic reason for the increase in crime and drug use. A strong family unit is able to overcome the temptations of society and stand as an example for others to follow.

Children are gifts from God and deserve to be treated as such. They are not given as pawns to use in a divorce settlement. They are not personal property; they are individuals with feelings and need the love of both parents in a loving home environment. All families have problems, but if all members involves are willing these problems can be overcome. Through overcoming, the family unit becomes stronger and therefore less susceptible to breaking up. It is up to the individuals involved in a marriage to make it work, no one else can do it for them. A close relationship with God and putting Him first in their relationship can ensure a successful marriage, one where the temptations of society cannot penetrate. All have temptations in their lives and those with a good understanding of God and what He wants for them will survive.

TIMES OF OLD

⸺⸺⟨⟨⟨⟩⟩⟩⸺⸺

As a nor'easter raged outside, the lights flicker and then go out. I fumble in the dark and find the lamp of old; it has set on the mantel filled and ready for such an occasion as this. Striking a match, I light its wick and the lamp comes to life. It fills the room with a flickering glow; it cast shadows on the wall as someone passes by it. As I sit back into my grandfather's chair within the flickering light, memories of times gone by come to mind.

I gathered the children around the fireplace to keep warm and told them of times when I was a child and we had no electricity or TV, only a crystal-radio. I recalled the times when father would cast shadows of animals and birds on the wall by the use of his hands between the lamp and the wall. Other times we would strain our ears to listen to the antics of Fibber Magee and Molly or the laughter of Mr. Guilder Sleeve as the crystal radio faded in and out. On Sunday nights, we listened to Charlie McCarthy and Mortimer Snerd or the antics of Amos and Andy as they portrayed the times in which we lived. The movie shows on Saturday afternoons where Roy Rogers rode his horse Trigger as he chased the bad men who always ended up in jail. When the morals of the movies were to portray that good overcomes bad and only limited violence was shown. Never a kiss did you see or disrobing of any kind. All of these memories and more came to mind as I rocked in grandpa's chair in the glow of the lamplight.

Times of when mothers stayed home and raised their families. Dad never had much money but we never went hungry either, we made do with what we had. Mother Nature created our playground where we learned to entertain ourselves. We had but a few material things but we did have a good sense of family, we looked forward to the holidays when all of our relatives and friends gathered to share each other's company and have a festive meal. Children, cousins and friends all sat around after the dishes were done and listened to the old folks spin tales of when they were young, tales of the sea, and of railroading or whatever their interests were. A time for children to be seen and not heard. Along with cousins and friends were raced and romped through the fields and woods playing Cowboys and Indians or hide and seek. Only going in the house long enough to eat. With our pockets filled with goodies, we ran and played after dark by the light of our flashlights. A fight now and again, but usually settled between ourselves, we dared not let our parents know for fear of being punished. We were always angels in our own eyes and would never start anything unless we thought that we could get away with it and not get caught.

When one of the adults came out and called us to come in, off to bed we went. If we were lucky one of our friends would stay overnight, and of course we would spend a sleepless night or so it seemed. If we made too much noise, either mom or dad would come to the stairs and quiet us down. Under the covers we would hide so that no one could find us or so we thought. The next day we would race and romp some more until it was time for our guests to go home.

When hay season came, we pitched hay from morning until night, stacked it high in the hayloft until it was full, we worked whether we liked it or not. It took all hands to keep things going in those days. The plowing was done by horse drawn equipment and that was shared often times between family and friends. Most of the field-work was done by hand and some of it by mine, no time to run and play as long as there was work to be done. It did however instill in us the value of work. At the end of summer, we received our school clothes as wages from the Sears and Roebucks catalog. We looked forward to receiving new clothes and shoes to wear to school, for during the summer we never wore shoes, except to go to Sunday school or some other special occasion.

Aunt Bessie and Uncle Roy lived in Boston and came and visited us occasionally, they drove what was called a touring car. It had a canvas top and windows made of mica. In the summertime, it was fun to ride in with the top down, but in the winter, it was cold and hard to keep warm. Mother would bundle us up in coats and blankets and wrapped hot bricks or stones in paper or cloth for us to put our feet on to keep them warm.

A trip to Boston to visit Aunt Bessie and Uncle Roy was always a special treat. Boston was almost a hundred miles from home; it took between four and five hours to drive that distance. Top speed was thirty five to forty miles per hour on narrow two-way roads. We would carry our lunch with us and only stopped if someone had to go to the bathroom or to get gas. There was a draw bridge over the Cape Cod cannel and ship travel was usually quite heavy, often we would have to stop and wait for a ship to pass before they world lower the bridge and allow traffic to continue. This was always a big treat to see big ships pass before us. We rode the trolley cars to the Franklin Park Zoo, which at the time was one of the best Zoos in the country. We were like children in a wonderland, with the trolley cars, streetlights, movie house close to their home and across the street from where they lived was a large wooded area where the Hobos gathered and lived in the woods. That was a spooky place and we were told never to go anywhere near that place or they might take us with them, we did not have to be told twice.

Uncle Roy worked in a candy factory, on one occasion I went to work with him for a day. We rode the trolley car to his place of work and I saw how candy was made. Before the day was over I had my pockets full of different kinds of candy, I thought that that was the best place anyone could work because one could have all of the candy that they could eat. As he introduced me to his fellow workers, I was rather shy and my handshake was like a wet dishrag. Uncle Roy was the one who taught me to shake hands like a man, (as he put it) with a firm grip, that I still do to this day.

In the winter on the farm, we used wood to heat the house, one of my jobs was to help father cut the wood into stove length pieces and then split it and stack it so that it could dry. We had a make and break engine to drive the saw, it was more commonly called a one-lunger, it only had one cylinder that fired about every other stroke unless it was under a load and then it fired every stroke. It had a four-inch wide leather belt that ran from the flywheel of the engine to the saw arbor. The saw arbor had babbitt bearings, which had to be kept oiled to keep them from wearing out as fast. One of my jobs was to take the wood away from the saw blade as father cut it. The saw blade was twenty four to thirty inches across and whined as it turned. You had to stand quite close to it as it was cutting the wood, one miss step or falter and you could lose a hand or a finger. One had to keep their mind on what they were doing. I have spent many a day cutting wood with it or helping dad cut wood. When cutting alone you let the cut pieces build up under the blade until they got in the way and then you very carefully removed the wood from under the blade.

To start the one-lunger you turned the flywheel by the means of a crank, which was a part of the flywheel until the engine fired. Sometimes it would backfire and kick back the wrong way and it felt like it would break your arm. Once going you slipped the drive belt onto the saw arbor and then put the other end on the flywheel of the engine, being careful not to get your hand or fingers caught in the belt. As you did this, you used a piece of wood to force the belt into its proper position. Then as the belt was turning, you applied some belt dressing to the belt to keep it from slipping. No one ever got hurt while running the saw rig, but I have known men who have lost fingers or hands either by getting them into the saw blade or the drive belt.

The time came when father wanted a tractor to make his work easier and enable him to cultivate more ground. He could not afford to buy one so he decided to make one. He bought an old truck and a small welder and proceeded to strip the truck down to its frame. He took the frame and configured it the way that he wanted it. He mounted the radiator and engine and then added a three-speed transmission in front of a four-speed transmission, then a short driveshaft to the rear wheels. He welded the truck seat in place, which completed the job. It was a crude looking tractor but it had more power than many of the modern ones. When he engaged both transmissions, it moved so slow that one could walk faster than the tractor would move. It had power enough to move a house off its foundation without spinning a wheel. He used a six-cylinder Chevrolet engine, which he rebuilt to power the tractor. He used this tractor for years until times got better and he could afford to buy a factory built tractor. He was proud of that tractor and well he should have been.

Father was like that, if he needed something and he could not afford to buy it, he built it from scratch. Like the time he wanted a boat for fishing and scalloping, he bought an old Catboat and rebuilt it. He installed a six-cylinder engine, bored the keel for the propeller shaft and when he finished remolding the Catboat he had one of the most seaworthy boats around. She was not very fast but you could go fishing or scalloping in most any kind of weather. When most of the boats could not leave harbor because of bad weather, the old Catboat could.

About then the lights came on and the TV began to blare. So comes to an end of telling tales of when I was young. The kids became more interested in the TV and lost interest in how I was brought up. Perhaps when the lights go out again they will want to hear more of how things used to be back in "the good old days".

I put the old lamp back in its place of honor with the book of matches by its side, ready for the next time when the lights went out. I sit back down in the same chair my grandfather used when he spun tales of his youth, my sisters and brother and I would listen intensely to his tales of old.

THE OLD BARN

The old barn I can still see. with its open doors, and hear the sounds of the cows from within.

Over its big door hung the sign, "Phillips Farm" for all to see.

During the summer, we filled its loft with sweet smelling hay for the winter to come.

In the loft, we did play hide and seek as we buried ourselves in its sweet smelling hay.

Cow stanchions all in a row on either side of the main floor.

They made their own noise as the cows moved from side to side.

They each had their own water cup from which the cows drank when it became their need.

We milked and fed them hay and grain twice a day.

Coming of spring, we turned them loose in the pasture to roam and eat the sweet grasses as they pleased.

In the morning and evening, we drove them back to the barn where we milked them by hand.

In the shed on the side of the barn was kept the tools and supplies that were needed to maintain the herd.

When the town fire siren went off, with the aid of a rope to the top of its roof we would climb, for the fire to find.

From this lofty perch, we could see far and wide, including the center of town and far at sea.

During the hunting season there has been many a deer hung from its lofty beams.

Spring, summer, winter, or fall there was always something to be done in that old barn on top of the hill.

When the winds blew strong, its timbers creaked and groaned just like a sailing ship far at sea.

It swayed and shook when the hurricanes did blow, but stand fast it did, I want everybody to know.

But, during one such storm it bowed to the wind that blew too strong.

On the ground it did lie, never to have its loft filled with that sweet smelling hay of years gone by.

Or, never to have cows within its shelter when the snows did fly.

All hearts were broken for in a heap to see it lie.

As much of a loss as it was, some of its timbers survived.

They were used to build a new barn, but not as big or as high.

The cows being gone there was no need for a loft, just a barn big enough to hold the farmers supplies.

A Smile

A smile is the outward appearance
of an inward glow.

A gift of friendship from one to
another.

A gift once given need never be
taken back.

It is given with no strings attached.

A parting of the lips in friendly
bliss.

It blesses the giver within their heart,
it warms the receiver to their
very soul.

It calms the fears of those who are
afraid.

A smile can chase the blues away,
it can change an enemy into
a friend.

Put them all together and what do
you have?

A joyous and friendly world in
which to live.

MEANING OF CHRISTMAS

The twinkling lights of Christmas shinning so
bright on a clear winter's night.

They represent the Yuletide season when Jesus
was born in a manger on a starry night.

It was God who came to earth that night of long
ago, He came to free mankind from their sins
and restore him in His sight.

Glory be to the one who came to free you and me,
praising His name is what Christmas
is all about.

Many seek to stand by his side, but unless their
heart is pure and clean, this will never be.

Jesus healed the sick and broken hearted and
gave His word to His followers to
ponder and store in their
hearts.

Bless us O Lord we pray, as through this life
we go, love us in spite of our sins.

Christmas may come but once a year, but
Jesus is here all year through to
help us life as one of His.

WHAT'S IN A NAME

Just the name of Jesus invokes thoughts of love,
purity, patience, healing, power,
Lamb and sacrifice.

Jesus came into this world meek as a Lamb
and expressed nothing but love for His
fellowman.

He was pure in thought and deed, He cared for
everyone, including you and me.

He preached His Father's ways and left it up to
you and me to apply it to our lives, O
what a blessing was He.

He healed the sick, made the blind to see, and
raised the dead from the grave.

He was and is the salvation of man, He freely
gave his life for the sins of the whole
world on the cross of Calvary.

Jesus was the sacrificial Lamb, in Him and
through Him all can come to the
cross and be saved.

As of old, just the mention of his name can
turn a sinner into a Saint in
the wink of an eye.

FAITH

To some faith is an attribute of God, to others
faith is not only an attribute of
God, it a way of life.

In my youth, I had self-will, when I grew older
I met God and now I do His will.

In death my eyes will be opened, then the glory
of God I will see.

When young I had strength to carry my daily
loads, now that I am old I have endurance.

When I was young, death was for the elderly,
but now that I am old, death is for
everyone, including me.

As a young man I sought knowledge, now that
I am old I seek wisdom.

Along my path of life I picked violets and gave
them to my mother, now I pick them
and put them on her grave.

I hope that one day someone will do the same
for me, for we are our brother's
keeper.

Through Faith we shall endure, through the
Cross we shall live and glorify our
Father in heaven.

WHICH WAY IS UP

As earth spins through the cosmos which way is up?
Is up to our left or is it to our right, or is it overhead,
or perhaps under our feet?

Are we standing upright, or are we standing on
our head?

Though our feet are on the ground, is our head on
top, or are we upside down?
Which way is up?

If we extend our arms over our heads, are they
pointing up or are they pointing down?

Is someone on the other side of the earth
standing upright or upside down?

Is up to the East, or to the West, or is to the
North or to the South?

Which way is up or is up upside down?

Would we get dizzy if we were upside down
while spinning around, we all cannot
be upright, or can we?

If this world stopped spinning would we fall
up, or would we fall down?

Are you confused or is it me, lets spin
around and see.

GARDEN GATE

There is a white picket fence along the side of
the road, with Hollyhocks so proud and
tall, they stand as sentinels on either
side of the garden gate.

The gate that opens wide when friends come
to call, it also beckons to strangers to
come inside and enjoy the friendship that no fence can hide.

Come in and sit a while, sip the tea that is
served with a smile to all who enter
through the garden gate.

If by chance, you find the garden gate
closed, open it wide, for all are
welcomed inside.

Before the cold of winter arrives, stop by,
sit a while, take in the beauty of
of fall, enjoy the hospitality
you will find behind
the garden gate.

THE WIND

O wind, where do you come from and where do you go?

I watch all day, I watch all night, I neither see you come
nor do I see you go.

I watch you ruffle the leaves on the trees and watch you
disturb the surface of the sea, and yet I see thee not.

The clouds you move hither and yon, sometimes you
touch the ground and blow us all-around.

I marvel at your strength, when the ships at sea you
blow about, is there nothing that you cannot
move from place to place?

You blow where you wish, you obey not the commands
of man, nor do you spare him when in your fury
you destroy everything in your way.

Sometimes you whisper and are gentle as a lamb. Other times you roar like a lion and raise havoc with man.

However there is one voice you obey, the same one I obey. The voice from heaven we both obey, for God holds this world in His hands and He is in command.

Signs Of Fall

First to arrive are the cool nights when we grab another blanket to keep us cozy and warm.

Then one morning we awake to find the ground covered with frost, a harbinger of what is to come.

With the rising of the sun, the frost disappears, but in our bones, we have the urgency to prepare for the winter to come, when the snows pile high and keeps us inside.

Time to pull the logs out of the woods, cut them up and stack the wood before the snows begin to fly.

Remembering that preparing the winter's wood warms you thrice, once when you cut the trees, once when you cut, split and stack the wood, and once when the stove turns cheery-red.

Then comes the night when a killing frost puts the flowers of the field to sleep till the coming of spring.

One by one, the leaves of the trees take on their fall colors, transforming the landscape into a collage of brilliant colors.

From the shrubs to the trees beauty abounds, not by the hand of man but a display of God's love for man.

Overhead the geese form their V formation, heading to warmer climes, Chipmunks scamper about gathering nuts to store for the winter to come.

The deer begin to herd and seek shelter deep in the forest till the coming of spring.

By the time the snows arrive, all are ready to face the winter ahead, then it will be time to ride snowmobiles through the snow covered fields and across the frozen lakes.

Those Who Mourn

⸻⟨∞⟩⸻

A time to wash away our cares with tears, a time to adjust to the loss of a loved one, it is those who are left behind who feel the sense of loss.

We weep for ourselves and console one another because we feel alone to face our daily trials.

Where have they gone, why did they have to die?

As much as we might prepare ourselves for the loss of a loved one, we are never ready to let our loved ones go. Go they must for it is the way of all flesh.

Rather we should rejoice for their work here on earth is done; now they can rest in peace in the arms of our Creator.

Jesus stands as a beacon and holds out His hand that we might find comfort on our journey home.

He speaks to our hearts and lets us know that we do not die; we just leave our mortal beings behind and step into a new live that was previously unseen.

We enter into a spiritual life where we are free from the cares of our earthly life and find comfort in the presence of our heavenly home.

A NEAR DEATH EXPERIENCE

⊸⧢⊷

A story told me by a friend of mine.

He experienced a heart attack (unknown to him), before the doctor resuscitated him, he found himself crossing a large field which had a lot of pretty wildflowers in it. The sky was rosy red and very peaceful. Off in the distance was a small village with well-kept homes. As he approached the village, he could hear the barking of dogs. The barking was of a friendly nature, meant to welcome all who approached. When he got close to the village, the residents came out of their houses to welcome him with open arms.

At this point, he heard other voices that turned out to be the doctors who were working over him. He awoke with the knowledge that death was nothing to fear; rather it was to be embraced as a transition from one life to another.

At this point in time that man has returned to that field of flowers and that village. He is now one those residents who came out and greeted him.

Embrace The Day With A Smile

———⌾———

When the alarm goes off, arise, go forth with
the expectation of a glorious day.

Look forward to the tasks that lie ahead,
greet your fellow worker with
a smile.

Complain not when asked to do a chore
that is not to your liking.

Do your job to the best of your ability,
let not your fellow workers
lead you astray.

When noon comes, give God thanks for
your meal and return to work
content.

Stand as a "Light" that shines in the
dark, exemplify the true meaning
of love towards your
fellowman.

Help those to the best of your ability
who ask it of you, go that extra
step without being told.

Spread no rumors lest you get caught
and have to pay the price for
spreading lies.

When it comes time to go home, leave
with peace between you and your
fellow worker.

When arriving home enter your house
with love in your heart for your
spouse and family.

Talk with God before going to sleep,
thank him for your day of labor
and for your family.

The Old Rocking Chair

I now sit on the porch and am motionless. It wasn't always that way, I have rocked more miles than most cars of my day.

I have heard many lovers pledge their love one to another as they swung in the hammock on the end of the porch.

I have given many a weary soul rest at the end of a long day. I have rock many a child to sleep at night and heard them repeat their evening prayers before falling off to sleep.

When the wind blew I rocked all by myself, I have been heard to say, "Come, sit on me and wile the time away, relax, fall asleep, no one will care."

Though I am now old and can no longer bear the weight that I once could, I am still willing to try, so come and sit on my seat and we will rock together till the break of day.

My joints are now weak from age, soon they will put me away and become a memory of old, but for now I am content to just sit here on the porch and let the wind help me rock back and forth.

THE LITTLE CHURCH ON THE CONOR OF ADAM AND HICKORY

⌘

The church on the corner of Adam and Hickory, Farina Ill.

When you enter in you are greeted with warm smiles and the friendly hands of those within.

Looking around you see just a plain and simple sanctuary, when the services begin they are conducted by just plain folks and you can feel their love for the Lord.

Pastor Don preaches the sermon of the day; it comes from his heart and soul, not from some print line.

The love for God is apparent and fills the sanctuary as the congregation sing hymns of praise to God above.

Upon leaving the service for the day one's hopes are renewed and one is ready to face the challenges of the coming days.

I have stood in the square where the Pope blesses all who are there; I have seen the beauty of the Sistine Chapel with all of its gold and treasures of old.

I have seen the ceiling that Michael Angelo painted while on his back, the huge cathedrals where their ceilings seem to touch the sky.

Where the organs boom forth their music that fills the whole sanctuary, it is all so glorious to see and hear.

But, I have yet to find a church so big and full of love as that little church on the corner of Adam and Hickory.

CHAPEL OF THE CROSS

———◇◈◇———

Standing majestically in a grove of tall pines, surrounded by cotton fields of old, secrets of the past echo within its walls.

The cemetery in the back holds the remains of those who built the CHAPEL OF THE CROSS during the years of slavery, lovers also have their place among the knurled cedars that now grace this place of rest.

Guarded by a rustic iron fence with a squeaky gate they sleep on till the day of resurrection.

On certain nights of the year when the moon is full and the smell of jasmine is in the air, one can hear the cries of the maiden who lost her lover in a duel for her hand in marriage, now side by side they lie silent in their graves.

Stories of old abound, restless souls wander the dark of night that conger up tales of love and tragedy.

In the days of old on the Sabbath the chapel bell sounded across the cotton fields and called all to come and hear the word of God, first the Masters of the plantations and them the indentured were required to hear in hopes of saving their souls.

The interior of the Chapel is rustic and simple with its high peaked ceiling and plank bottom pews, special pews for the elite that no one else could use. With the sun streaming through the windows, the sanctuary takes on an air of antiquity.

If one sits quietly in a pew of the old Chapel, they can still hear the weekly sermons echoing among the rafters, but silent are the cries of those who were unjustly treated and came to this old Chapel for mercy to seek.

The storms over the years have taken their toll on the CHAPEL OF THE CROSS, but it is still sound and for generations yet it will be a place to visit and listen to the tales of old.

For now, listen for the bell in the CHAPEL OF THE CROSS ring on the Sabbath, calling all to reverence its past.

Remembered Love

On wings of love, I flew through the darkness of the night, into my lover's arms I cannot wait to be. Just the thoughts of her love fills my heart with joy.

It has been way too long since I have felt her passionate lips press against mine.

In my mind, I have already landed and am headed to my lover's arms, even though the plane has many miles yet to go.

My thoughts run on ahead, as in my mind I see her tender face, the smell of her perfume lingers still, "I love you my darling" echoes in my ears.

Her prying eyes make my heart beat faster, I can feel the love that she has for me.

We will curl up on the couch in front of a warm fire and caress one another so tenderly. The lights will be low, our special music we will play on this night of nights.

The crackling fire will cast shadows of love as we passionately embrace, our hearts will beat as one, our souls will be at peace, nothing could spoil or take away from the love that we will share this night.

Romance is in the air, soon it will be fulfilled; my love and I will always hold this night dear in our hearts as we embrace. It will warm us through and through as the years go by, as through life we will go hand in hand.

Every anniversary, no matter how old, we will cherish the thoughts of bliss that we shared on the night that we wed.

Oh my love, it is a though it were yesterday when we held one another so close and our love was new.

Now it is time to say good-bye, for in your grave you lay, be patient my love. It will not be long before once again, we will be in each other's arms and our hearts will once again beat as one.